NESI L STONE

Split Between Magic

First edition

ISBN: 979-8-89587-329-8

Editing by Cover to Cover edits

This book was professionally typeset on Reedsy.
Find out more at reedsy.com

Let your rage spark a flame and your tears fuel the fire.

burn it all down

for a woman's rage spreads like wildfire

Also By Nesi L Stone

Broken Moon Spirit

Trigger Warnings

This book contains matters not suitable
for audience under 18.

Between these pages you will not find a sweet book about a
woman finding her place in the world; what you will find is a
dark book about a woman screaming her rage at the world.
You have been warned.

Death
Chapter 33

Night Terrors
Chapters 4, 13, 19, 20, 32

Drowning
Prologue
Chapter 14

Explicit Language
Chapters 5, 12, 18, 20, 24, 32, 37, 40, 41

Explicit Sexual Acts
Chapters 24, 32, 40

Genocide
Chapters 6, 29

Rape
Chapter 26

Grief
Chapters 29, 33

Emetophobia
Chapters 19, 39

These themes are found through out the story as a whole.
While this is not an exhaustive list of chapters; the listed
chapters have heavily prevalent in that chapter.

Playlist

High Road by Koe Wetzel & Jessie Murph

Cut by Maren Morris feat. Julia Michaels

Anatomy by Kenzie

Fictional by Khloe Rose

The Fruits by Paris Paloma

Battle Scars by Guy Sebastian feat. Lupe Fiasco

Hold Me by Zoe Wees

I'd Rather Overdose (Remix) by honestav feat. Mod Sun

Battlefield by SkyDxddy

Care About Me by JESSIA

Reviews for Split Between Magic

Prologue

The darkness watched her, holding its breath. as she clawed at the empty space. She wasn't falling but there was no ground found under her feet. Her small lungs screamed, fighting to be, to take in air where there was none. She gave up clawing at the darkness, her small fingers digging at the unmarred skin of her throat, leaving long, angry welts. The darkness around her breathed in, taking in what she was. *Delicious.* The presence in the darkness got closer, taking in the child; fighting like a wild animal. *So fragile.* The child stopped, looking back at the darkness itself, reaching out a hand towards it, welcoming it. The darkness felt her small fingers gently caress it.

My little monster.

The darkness hissed, tightening its grip on the girl, as a burning hand plunged through it. *No! Mine! My little monster.* The darkness reached out, a gentle wisp of darkness, turned to smoke, and then a clawed hand. The darkness reached out, grabbing the child's foot at the same time as the hand grabbed her wrist. The child gripped the hand as it pulled her up and out, her little fingers trailing through the darkness stroking it goodbye.

This isn't goodbye, little monster....

I

Coming

The spark fought against the night.

1

Nodin huffed, blowing the hair out of her face. It had been escaping her bun for the last hour. Sorting her life into what she could travel with -which was a suitcase and a backpack- had been an impossible endeavor. She had been putting it off for weeks. Staring at her overstuffed suitcase in the middle of the floor she reassessed. Finally deciding to start over, she tipped it on its back, onto the floor. Start with the most important, then slowly work back from there. Nodin packed her journal, then two more empty ones, followed by her writing supplies. Then several of her favorite books, only ones she knew she'd read over and over. *So much to learn.*

Personal possessions filled up the suitcase, followed by clothes and soaps, all the unloved, but needed life tools. Sitting on the top of the suitcase, she zipped it closed, the metal of the zipper digging into her fingers as she worked it along the thread. She sat back on her heels taking one last look at the cabin she had spent all the early years of her life in. How it had grown with her in the last decade.

She ran her fingers over the wall of books, all the familiar titles, one last time before marching out the front door. On the threshold, she turned back, waving her fingers through the air, pulling the weave with her, causing it to float through the house. She closed the door as vines started climbing up the walls, returning the house to the wilds it had once been.

The two days of travel started with a spark in her heart and turned to a relished burn in her bones as time went on. It wasn't until she was mere hours from the city did the wilds part into a tamer, paler, mortal version of nature. One that wasn't dark and wild, one that lost its soul in exchange for a cookie-cutter beauty. Nature, all neat and within its assigned places. A mortal version. It pulled at her heart, like a declawed cat, safe for those around it -but a crippled version of its past.

Nodin felt the difference in the air around her when she made it to the city, like dust coating her skin. She looked around at all the buildings, reaching like claws into the sky, as though they could take over everything that was once there. A metal plague. Tilting her head back to peek at the little wisps of blue, she could see between the gray walls that boxed her in -it looked down at the small wild animal that had wandered into its open jaws.

Nodin walked through the streets till she found the one she was looking for, feeling more disconnected from everything around her with each step. The city grinding her up in its teeth. Pushing on the large wooden door she stumbled into the cold void. The room was empty, shy of a single desk, with a bat-like woman sitting at it.

"Name?" she rasped with a voice that sounded on the better end of a pack a day. She blinked at her from behind her thick glasses perched on her too-long nose. The frames stuck out from her thin face in an idiosyncratic juxtaposition. "I'm here for the entrance exam." She held her ground waiting for the woman to do something. "Name?" The lady repeated. "Nodin Merle," Nodin recited. "Middle name?" the lady still didn't look at her. "Solace," Nodin fidgeted nervously. "Now what exam did you want to take?" She shuffled the papers on her desk around.

Nodin watched as she moved the same papers from one place, then back again. "Briggems." The ladies' eyes finally looked up at her. "First door on your left." She pointed to the door with one long finger after she gave Nodin a once-over. Taking a breath to settle her nerves, Nodin turned on the balls of her feet and trotted over to the door. "You can't bring those bags in there," the woman called as Nodin reached the door. Silently, Nodin shuffled her bags against the wall outside the room. She smoothed down her cotton shirt before stepping through the doorway.

~

The written exam left Nodin's mind feeling numb, and her fingers feeling stiff, covered in smudged ink. Nodin sat in silence as the short plump woman graded her exam. She wasn't left waiting long. "As you know my dear, a passing grade is a score of 80 points or higher. You got 81 points." The woman smiled warmly at her, it lit up her whole face. It lit up her soul.

She gave off the feeling she was gonna offer Nodin a loaf of fresh bread at any time. "Please head through those doors to the practical exam, my dear." She waved her hand through the air like she was conducting a musician. With her head floating like a cloud in the grasp of a strong breeze, Nodin floated towards the door.

A small woman sat at a round table. Her short brown hair and large eyes gave off the feeling of dappled sunlight in a clearing. She may have had some pixie blood in her family somewhere. The table was small, no more than a side table really, in the middle was a large object hidden under a black cloth. The object seemed to pulse, reaching out, probing the world around it. "My latecomer." The woman's voice was soft, floating to her ears like a petal on the wind. "Please sit."

Nodin perched at the edge of her seat, eyeing the object as it seemed to hum at her. *Like calling to like.* The practitioner pulled the cloth off the table, under it sat a white rock. It was translucent, white smoke swirling under the surface, little wisps of color dancing with the smoke, pink, orange, blue, swirling through the stone.

"Please place your hands on the top." Her voice was like bells. Nodin looked at the stone, Nodin's fingers twitched as she tried to unravel the mystery before her. The rock hummed and a sputtering, a glow bloomed in the depths of the rock. "It won't hurt you, it just tests the strength of your magic," the woman cooed quietly. Nodin held her breath as she steeled her nerves, cutting herself off of the weave almost completely. Setting her hands lightly on the stone she waited, feeling its rough texture under her hands. It hummed at her in disapproval, sensing how deep her magic truly ran. It seemed to hiss at her, naming her the liar she was. The rock took her in, all that she was, all that she could be -drinking her in like fresh lemonade on a hot day. It chewed on her, thinking, before spitting her out.

The stone flickered to life; a glow pulsing, growing brighter and brighter, flickering like a dance. The woman hummed. Nodin took her hands off of the rock looking at the woman. The glow persisted for a few seconds, a thousand heart beats contained within it. Slowly, the rock dimmed, whispering to Nodin as it faded. The woman threw the cloth back over the rock with a sharp flick of her wrist. She smiled at Nodin.

"Congrats! You have passed. Just in the nick of time." The woman stood up and handed Nodin a large package of papers encased in a flimsy paper folder. "How well did I do?" Nodin asked, her hand grasping the papers. "We don't disclose that information." The woman didn't let go of the papers, holding her gaze. "Understood." Nodin pulled gently at the papers. "But what I will say is this; you will have to work hard in school to stay. You can't rely on raw talent to make it through." The woman let go of the papers, turning to flounce out the door without another word.

Nodin stood still looking at the table. She threw a glance over her shoulder before tugging the cloth off the stone in one strong movement. Nodin regarded the stone; it was silent. She gently placed a single finger on its milky surface. Instantly, the stone went cold, flooded with dark gray taking over the opalescent white. Quickly, the rock tumbled past gray to black, turning opaque; black swallowing all the light in the room. "Hello, little monster," the stone whispered to her. Startled, Nodin ripped her hand back from the rock. It faded back to its natural milky light the farther she pulled her hand away.

"Stay safe. Child of darkness." It whispered goodbye as Nodin ran from the room. She snatched her bags from the lobby and stormed out of the building. Nodin ran, a blur of false orange lights and gray dancing in her tear-stained vision. Finally, she came to a stop at the base of a massive oak tree. It sat in the middle of a large courtyard, in a square of dirt barely bigger than its trunk.

Nodin laid her hand on the bark of the tree, her fingers dipping into the deep divots in the bark. As her skin brushed its rough exterior, the tree grounded her on the deepest level. Her soul opened up its lungs and took a deep breath it had been holding since she left her home. The old tree was withering and gnarly, the tree choking on the suffocating city, its knotted roots carving out its defiant existence.

She could do this. Nodin settled at the base of the tree, her back leaning against its firm trunk. For the first time, she turned her mind to the interior of the packet. A generic letter of acceptance to Briggems sat on top, on thick card stock paper, underneath it sat a whole pile of paperwork. The longest questionnaire Nodin had ever seen. The curling type at the top of the first page stated:

Please complete before boarding the train. Please turn over to the Ticketmaster upon boarding.

1

Nodin buckled down, pen in hand, and attacked the questions. Nodin flew through them, not looking up, page after page. Flipping over the last one, she finally looked up, the little slivers of sky peeking out from behind the skyrises painted orange.

Sorting her way through identical building after building in a maze of mirrors, Nodin finally made it to the train station and to the platform where the train sat puffing smog into the air. "Last call!" a ticket master yelled from beside the train, his buttoned uniform crisp sporting the rail company's logo. Nodin scuttled over to him, flourishing her packet of papers in the air.

He glanced through them, thumbing from page to page. "Test taken… Today. Do you like living life with not a second to spare? This is the last train to Briggems. Ms…Merle. Ms Merle." He swung the door open for her. Nodin turned to drag her suitcase onto the train. The man tutted at her picking up her overstuffed bag like it was a small briefcase. Clambering into the carriage of the train, after the man and her suitcase, she made her way down the narrow hall, the only light was the sun that filtered through the outer windows. The whole carriage was made up of small roomettes, with sliding doors.

Nodin passed several empty roomettes before she came across one with another person in it. She made her way to the two roomettes that straddled the very back of the carriage: one was empty, and one had its curtains drawn. Folding herself into the last empty one, Nodin sat with her legs tucked under her, her head resting on the window pane. It wasn't long before the train pulled out of the station, and as it dove deep into the forest outside the city, it started to rain.

Time was marked by fat droplets of water rolling down the window, thundering on the roof above her. It didn't take long for the sound of the rain to wrap her up in its gentle arms as she drifted to sleep. Nodin nestled in her dreams like a baby animal in the sanctuary of the roots of a tree, the gentle fingers of darkness stroking her mind hungrily.

Nodin woke up to the train slowing down, her body stiff. She uncurled her legs, blood rushing to them. She almost toppled over as pain shot through her calves. The speaker crackled on announcing their arrival, informing the passengers to *'remain seated till directed to exit by a staff member.'*

Nodin pulled her mane of hair out of the rat's nest it was currently tangled into and ran her fingers through it, looping it back into the claw clip as neatly as she could with no mirror. Nodin sat in her seat rubbing her legs waiting, her backpack resting on the top of her suitcase that had appeared in her roomette when had been sleeping.

"For you." A blonde woman in the rail company's uniform tugged open the door to her roomette. She held out an identical packet of papers to her, this time made of nicer paper, and embossed with Briggems school emblem. *Ab uno disce omnes;* from one learn all. Nodin argued with her suitcase all the way down the hallway and out of the train. Several people were swiftly exiting the station, already in school uniforms and lacking the packet currently tucked under Nodin's arm. Several roads branched off from the platform, each with people walking down them, giving no insight as to which one she should take.

Resting half butt cheek on the edge of her suitcase she ruffled through her packet. Sitting on the top was a map, guiding her to the school. Keeping her nose in the packet, Nodin made her way down the road towards the school. Under that map were two more maps; one labeled class room guide, and the next dorm guide. On the back of the dorm guide was a bunch of information; dorm room number and how to unlock the door. Flipping over the map of the class guide, her class schedule was laid out. The last page being the code of conduct.

Code of Conduct

All classes are mandatory

No unathorized departure
of school property is
prohibited.

Cheating and plagerism is
prohibited

The use of unathoriezed raw
magic is prohibited
No causing harm to faculty or
students

Any illegal activity will be
reported to the athorities
imediately.
Each Professor may set
their own guidlelines and
rules for each class.

Headmaster and
Professors may add
addictional guidelines at
any time

Conduct yourselves accordingly

2

It took Nodin nearly an hour to find her dorm. Not only was the school huge, but it was old and filled with winding halls. She ran into several rooms that were not on the map, and two halls that were on the map, but nowhere to be found.

Finally at the door of her dorm room, she noted it was on the other side of the school than her classes. Nodin huffed bracing herself, she knocked on the door, three raps, nice and strong. "Coming!" an airy voice called from behind the door. A girl Nodin could only describe as a cloud greeted her in the door frame. Her light blonde hair, danced around her ears, floating around her head as though she had lost a fight with gravity. She wore a long white dress, the shape of which could only be defined as a wide triangle. "Welcome," she said in an almost song-like voice.

"I'm your roommate. Nodin Merle." Nodin flapped her pile of papers at her in explanation. "Ascelin." The woman before her gave no last name. "Please, come in." Ascelin waved her in, stepping back.

Nodin stepped through the threshold, glancing around. Despite the square walls of the hallway she had been stalking through, this room was circular, as if the door was in a tower. Despite being carved from the same rough stone as the rest of the school this room radiated warmth. "You are the last roommate," Ascelin said as she skipped past Nodin. "This is Willow, and that is Odette." She pointed to the two remaining girls, each of whom sat on a different plump couch.

The other girls looked up; Willow reminded Nodin of sunlight shining through amber. A tall woman with soft curves, which she had draped in silk pajamas, her warm honey-colored hair wrapped up in a crown around the back of her head. She sat up and looked over at Nodin, smiling. She changed position, leaving much of her ample body on show, miles of warm tan skin.

Odette got up, her thick black hair falling in a sheet behind her, her smile lighting up her porcelain skin. She was a small woman in contrast to Willow who sat next to her. She was wrapped in a bright satin robe, the pattern reminiscent of the northern continents. She blinked at Nodin, taking her in. All three women just looked at her waiting. "As I told Ascelin, I'm Nodin." She left out my last name this time as no one else had used theirs. "It's good to meet you." Odette had a loud voice that did not match her petite appearance.

Willow joined Odette on the couch, their fingertips brushing in some unspoken communication. "We already took our rooms as we got here two days ago," Willow announced, rubbing her arm. "I mean it wouldn't be that hard to move if you really cared…" Ascelin offered quietly. "No. No, I'm not picky." Nodin looked around, spotting five doors around the room.

Laid out before her was a cozy living room. The couches and chairs encircled a squat table before a large fireplace. Every inch of the stone walls was covered with large, thick tapestries. Each one was a scene surrounding a building, some with trees, some with rivers, all made from thick cloth designed to retain heat. "It gets cold here?" Nodin mused. "At night? Very," Willow answered. "It's really not that bad," Ascelin said, nudging Willow's side.

"This one is yours." Odette pointed to the sturdy door on the far right. "That one is the bathroom," Willow said pointing to the door opposite the entrance. "It's no more than a toilet and a sink," Odette muttered. "And none of us have yet to find a bathroom to bathe in," Ascelin said, with a grim expression.

"There has to be one somewhere." Odette's dark eyes flashed with an unrecognizable emotion. Nodin was still trying to decipher Odette's look when Willow walked over to the bathroom, swinging the door open to show her. "See?" Willow barked, startling Nodin out of her trance.

"It's not so bad," Nodin commented. "Now, in there, it gets cold at night," Ascelin muttered tersely, shivering at the thought. It took the four of them a little over an hour to settle into a happy peace. The girls were curled up, two each to a couch; Willow and Odette on one, and Nodin and Ascelin on the other. Willow hugged one of the many pillows to her chest, her legs splayed out on the table. Odette was spread-eagled over the arm of the couch. Nodin watched each woman so at ease with themselves. Taking up all the space they need, unapologeticly.

Odette stretched out, placing her feet on Willow's leg. Ascelin was wrapped in a large fluffy blanket she had dragged from her room. Ascelin had begged Nodin to let her braid her hair, and Nodin didn't mind the two thick loose braids that now hung down her back. Especially since Ascelin had given her a head massage with some rosemary oil beforehand, which had earned Ascelin giving everyone a massage. Willow opted out of the rosemary oil.

Nodin excused herself from the giggling mess they had all become, wheeling her suitcase into her empty room. It was a cold that quickly sank into her bones within seconds. Her teeth chattering, she rubbed her hands together, taking in the walls that would be her home for the next couple of years.

Sitting down on the floor she let her heart beat slow, breathing in the feeling of the room. The quiet echoed through her bones, replacing the heat of her blood -that the lively conversation in the other room had heated. Despite her enjoyment of her roommates, Nodin was a lonely soul, meant to be solitary, in the woods.

A small bed sat by the window, its white sheets crisp, the corners sharply folded. A slab of stone with four metal legs stood by the bed, a simple lamp sitting on it. Across from the door sat a small desk, with a chair tucked under it. Sat on the desk was a pile of clothes, her school uniform. A small closet was cut into the wall with a single bar across the top, not a single hanger in sight. The bare bones of a home. Walking over to the desk Nodin ran her fingers over the wood, it was untreated oak. Gently teasing the weave a small branch sprouted from the wood winding up. Little bark-covered vines sprung out of the branch forming a living shelf.

Tipping over the suitcase onto the floor. Nodin fiddled with the zipper it bounced open, spilling her clothes all over the floor. Nodin pulled her books from the mess and placed them on the shelf, leaving her notebooks on the desk. On the side table, she set a small trinket tray. Sorting through the few possessions she had brought, she took her time to find their perfect home.

Slowly, the room started to feel like home. With vines climbing the furniture, plants spider-webbed out from the window, and moss covered the stone walls, and her bed was piled high with her many blankets. Her backpack sat in her now empty suitcase, residing at the bottom of her closet. Her clothing was piled on top of the suitcase shy of her new school uniform.

3

Nodin curled up in her nest of blankets reading one of her favorite philosophical works. Authored over a hundred years ago, it held points of thought that had only become more prevalent in the recent years. Nodin spent her time frowning at the words on the page, biting on the edge of the blanket. A soft knock broke her focus and her door swung open. Ascelin peeked into the darkness of her room.

"It's easier to read with light," she noted, squinting at Nodin. Nodin picked up her candle off of the side table. "Got some." Ascelin shook her head with a little giggle bubbling up. "Dinner is almost over," she informed Nodin. "And where would I find this dinner?" Nodin set her book down, pulling out her maps. "In the dining hall. I can show you." Ascelin held out her slim hand. It almost glowed in the light of the candle, a ghostly metacarpus.

Nodin followed Ascelin through several halls, down many stairs, and almost to the main doors before heading deeper into the school. Before her stood massive doors, dark and twisted cherry wood, rising to the vaulted ceiling. "Here we

20

are." Ascelin flourished her hands at the doors. As Nodin stepped closer, the doors swung open, and several students in their uniforms strolled out, talking with each other. The school logo, a rose with thorns, was blue and not the gray of her uniform.

They were definitely not first years, though several of them looked younger than Nodin herself. With no age requirement on either end of the spectrum, the only admission requirement being the entrance exam the school was filled with all ages. "See you in class tomorrow." Ascelin bounced off down a different hall than the one they had just come down.

Taking in the hall before her, it sent Nodin's mind for a spin. The room was littered with wooden tables of different shapes and sizes, and chairs scattered about the tables. It was a mess with food waste, and soiled plates abandoned on all the tables, it was clearly the end of dinner. At the far end of the hall was one long table, covered in platters of food. Despite the mess of the well-used dining hall, the platters seemed untouched. *Such an unnecessary abundance of food.*

What caught Nodin's attention more than the feast was the wall behind the table. It looked to be a single sold gold sheet, shining and flickering in the light, but not reflecting the room at all. Little lights dancing on the surface.

While it was a solid single piece of mental, not a seam in sight, it had waves in it, digs and folds, like a sheet had been hung over a painting. Nodin turned from the wall to the table of food. Nodin picked through each item dismissing each one.

Great health choices, full of whole ingredients, nothing like some of the icky school meals Nodin had read about from other schools. All amazing home-cooked meals.

No neon orange pasta salad with hot dog pieces. Nodin filled her plate with a gorgeous salad filled with carrots, spinach, fig, and pickled beetroot, and other bright vegetables that she could not name. A stack of fresh, still warm, sourdough bread on the side. Nodin wandered through the hall trying to find a table to sit at. Several students darted in to get food after her, filling their plates and sitting at the closest tables before digging in greedily.

Nodin found a small table tucked in the corner by the door, perfect for a single person. Setting her heaping plate on the table, she settled down on a plain wooden chair. As Nodin was digging into the warm bread before it could cool down, a pair of young men came running into the dining room laughing; it filled the space with a chaotic clattering.

They loaded up boxes and boxes with food. Some of their boxes were nice glass and metal containers, some seemed to be reused takeout cardboard boxes. Once they'd been filled and packed into their bags they started to leave.

One of the young men grabbed a piece of steak off the buffet table, tilting his head back, dropping the meat into his mouth. Looking up, he winked at Nodin before following his friend back out the hall. Nodin grimaced at him; she couldn't believe that just the two of them needed that much food. Picking at the rest of her salad, moving bits of beetroot around her plate, she smeared red all over the white porcelain.

She shoveled the rest of her salad into her mouth, chewing it aggressively as she placed her plate and utensils in one of the many gray buckets of soapy water. Swallowing the last of the salad, Nodin left the dining hall, retracing her steps back to her dorm. The halls were lit by strips of glowing stone running along the bottom of the walls. Bending down, she ran a finger over the stone. It was smooth and cool to the touch. The glow stayed steady to her touch. Though at first Nodin suspected it had been the same stone as the entrance exam, she had been wrong.

Quietly slipping into her dorm, she weaved through the now empty couches, the fire burned down to red glowing coals. She paused before her door: she could hear the soft laugh of Willow coming from Odette's room. "You are back." Ascelin rubbed her eyes, peeking out of her room. "Goodnight," Nodin whispered. Turning to enter her room, she threw one last glance at Odette's door as both girls laughed. "They are anamchara," Ascelin said, looking at Odette's room. Nodin just hummed at her before disappearing into her room.

She kicked off her shoes, leaving them abandoned where they fell. Nodin dropped her clothes in a pile at the foot of her bed, slipping into her well worn-night slip. *Soul friends.* Ascelin may be right. Curling up in the tangle of blankets that made up her nest, Nodin slipped into a warm, dreamless sleep.

4

Hello, little monster. The darkness whispered into her sleeping mind. Nodin jumped awake, the sound of long claws scraping the stone ground echoing through her ears. Nodin held her breath, waiting to see if the sound would come again, if it was in fact real. Nodin shifted looking around, shaking the ghastly sound from her nightmare foggy mind. Peeling herself from her layers of bedding Nodin felt tired.

She hissed at the chill that ran up her legs as her feet hit the stone floor. *A rug.* Nodin needed a rug. It was well before the winter season, over a month before it hit. If the floor was this cold now, what would it be like in two months as they fought through the depths of winter?

Tossing her night slip on the bed, Nodin started to get ready for the day. Slipping into her underthings and a pair of thin stockings, she turned to her school uniform. Nodin frowned at the blouse, running her fingers over it. It was satin, a pale tan. Underneath the blouse was a knee-length gored skirt, the thick fabric was rough compared to the gentle satin blouse. At least the skirt had deep pockets in the sides. A shiny black lavalliere to be knotted at her decolletage. Nodin snarled slightly at the knitted cardigan, it may have matched the deep gray of the skirt but it was yet again a different textured fabric. All different textures.

On the breast pocket of the cardigan was the school's emblem and motto embroidered in gray thread. Nodin brushed the rose, tracing the letters in the words. *Ab uno desire omens.* "From one, learn all," Nodin whispered to the walls. Plain black socks and her well-worn leather shoes left her feet the only comfortable part of her body. Nodin slung the black cloak over her shoulders. She felt like a wild blackberry bush wrapped in chicken wire.

Tucking a pen in her left pocket, Nodin tucked a fresh notebook under her arm, the school maps clutched in her fist. Storming out of her room, Nodin swept through the living room about to leave. "Nodin!" Ascelin called from beside the empty fireplace. "We were gonna grab breakfast then head to class," Willow offered with a smile. *Breakfast.* Nodin looked down at her grumbling tummy. "Sounds good." Nodin fell into step with Willow as Odette and Ascelin talked, leading the way back to the dining hall. This time, the room was packed with chattering students. Weaving through hundreds of bodies the four of them made it to the buffet table. Ascelin leaned over and tried to say something over the noise. "LET'S GET FOOD AND GET OUT!" Ascelin shouted at them, nodding at each woman, before grabbing a of couple items they could eat while walking.

Snatching up a banana and an apple, sticking an oat flapjack into her mouth, Nodin groaned in pleasure at the sight of the end of the table. Hot drinks and travel mugs. The warm toasted scent of coffee wafted over her. Grabbing the metal tumbler, she filled it up with the dark and rich hot cocoa. It was made in the traditional southern hot cocoa by melting chocolate in coconut cream and then spiced. Nodin was tempted to grab another mug but Ascelin tugged on her elbow. All the women sported the metal travel mugs, each filled with a different drink. Ascelin had a mocha topped with whipped-cream and shaved chocolate flakes; Odette had a spiced latte; Willow had an iced espresso shot that she topped with a large amount of lavender-flavored cream.

Nodin blew lightly on her cocoa, sipping at it even when it burned her tongue. The deep rich flavor tasting of winter nights as a child. Her father had spent one particularly cold winter teaching her and how to make the drink, how to change the spices to aid in health. "What are everyone's first classes?" Willow asked from behind her. Ascelin had a small smear of whipped cream on her lip. "Introduction to casting, with Professor Manc, in room seven twelve," Ascelin answered, the cream still on her face. Nodin nodded at her. "Same." echoed Willow and Odette. Chatting between bites of food, and sips of their drinks the four women made their way to their first class.

The room was set up like an amphitheater, benches and desks circling a small circle of plush red carpet. A middle-aged man stood in the circle, leaning against the bottom row of desks talking to a group of students. Ascelin bid them goodbye before skipping off to fight through a crowd of people to join two other students sitting near the front. Ascelin chatted with them easily, the twins smiling at her. Willow and Odette found seats near the middle.

Nodin turned and climbed up the stairs, finding an empty row that almost brushed the ceiling. Sitting down, she watched the room fill up with many students all wearing crisp clean uniforms.

The professor stood up and walked into the center of the room, with a wave of his hand the lights dimmed, and the room fell silent. He turned on his heels taking in the class before him. "At the end of your time here you will graduate, if you graduate, with a mastery of the aspect of your choice." The professor's deep voice filled the room, sounding rich and full. "Choosing your aspect is not a simple task, the aspect you pick will define everything about you." The professor paced in a small circle, the pitch and volume of his voice staying steady. "You will not be alone in this endeavor. The years here will prepare you to make that choice. You will make this choice at the beginning of your third year here."

The professor spent two hours discussing what they would be learning this year, dismissing them with forty-five minutes till Nodin's next class. As the professor walked out, everyone stood and started to talk with each other, mingling with many different groups. Nodin darted out of the class, heading back to the dining hall. The halls were packed with students, all heading in different directions.

A few people were milling around the dining hall talking, catching up with classmates that they hadn't seen in weeks. Jetting towards the buffet table which had been cleared of breakfast and now was covered in snacks; Nodin let out a sigh seeing the drinks station was still there. Depositing her now-empty mug into a soup bucket, she headed to get another mug of cocoa.

Nodin made her way to her next class. Year One Decoction. It took Nodin almost the entire forty-five minutes to find her class. The tall pump professor who taught the class had them start an infusion for an ingredient they would need in their final exam at the end of the year. Nodin fled the warm room, the jar of her infusion tucked under her arm. She would need a book bag soon.

As she now had to carry three textbooks, her notebook, and a jar. Nodin rushed to her dorm as she had two hours for lunch. Setting the jar on her windowsill, she left her books on her desk. The reality of her situation settled on her; four years of her life where she would be scrutinized and monitored regularly, four years restricted to the abomination the mortals passed for casting. Four years to keep her identity secret. Then complete freedom. *Freedom.*

5

Ascelin burst through the door, her hands flapping about in the air. "Nodin!" she called, walking around the living room. "Lunch?" Ascelin paused in her pacing looking at her. "Willow and Odette are getting a table." Ascelin tossed her books onto the couch. She had pulled off her lavalliere, tying it around her head instead. Ascelin had lasted for only a handful of hours before modifying her uniform. Nodin guessed it was only the beginning of Ascelin's rebellion against the suffocating dress code.

Ascelin twittered about her class that she didn't share with Nodin all the way to lunch. Lunch was much tamer than breakfast had been, with students having a long break in the middle of the day. Willow waved them over to the table they had snagged, Odette was off at the buffet table grabbing two plates of food.

Nodin sat down with Willow while Ascelin went to join Odette. In the mere minutes that Odette and Ascelin were gone, three people asked if they could sit with them. Willow dismissed them all quickly with only a few words. Odette plopped next to Willow, setting a tray with a large bowl of chili, with sour cream and shredded cheddar piled on top.

"Oh, thank you," Willow cooed at Odette. Ascelin sat down with a spread of Alfredo chicken with garlic asparagus. Nodin left the three of them to eat as she meandered along the buffet table. She grabbed a bowl of spicy ginger and carrot soup, and some of the garlic asparagus. Much to Nodin's dismay, the hot cocoa was gone, replaced by a large assortment of juices.

Balancing a cup of juice, her soup bowl, and the plate of asparagus, she made her way back to the table. Everyone settled into the comfortable conversation of the table, everyone talking around mouthfuls of food. As lunch started to wind down, all the plates on their table long empty, a group of students walked into the dining hall. Nodin watched them walk into the room, a small group of men, surrounded by a larger group of followers. The mix of colors on their school uniforms labeled them as third years.

"Are they who I think they are?" Odette whispered, as all the women watched the group move deep into the hall. "Yes," Ascelin breathed. "Who?" Nodin turned to Ascelin. "The Heirs," Willow answered. "Heirs?" Nodin searched her mind as to who the group could be. "They are the named Heirs of the Six Families," Ascelin explained not looking away from them.

"They will end up ruling the continent, each will inherit one of the six governing seats." Finally, it clicked in Nodin's mind. She had been thinking too small. They were the ruling class. *The power they hold.* She watched them, pampered spoiled brats, raised with a silver spoon in their mouths. Raised to continue the destruction of the world around them, clinging to the power and control their families had stolen generations ago. Choke on the damn silver spoon in their mouths.

"They all came to this school at the same time?" Willow mused. "It's tradition," Odette countered. "See those two there?" Ascelin pointed to the two in the middle. "He's their leader, Ivor Daunte, but that guy next to him is Roman Van'Hight, he could be the leader if he wanted to." Ascelin pointed to the two men explaining the 'who's who.' "It's said he's more focused on school than politics," Willow chipped in. "The two on the left are Clovis Mandora, and Vane Potman. Behind them is Elijah Bakhart, and on the right is Remus Hoewlman." Ascelin continued to watch them as they made it to the buffet table. "They are all boys," Nodin noted.

"They are men," Ascelin corrected, not removing her eyes from them. "They are boys," Nodin corrected, wrinkling her nose at them. "Technically, each current seat holder can name any of their children as their Heir, however, yes this time they are all *boys*." Willow's voice dropped pointedly on boys, looking at Nodin. "Have fun in Herbology, the professor's a nut ball," Ascelin said in her sing-song voice as Nodin got up to leave. "I'd take some layers off," Nodin answered her, smiling.

The group of women all left together, as the Herbology class the other three had been in when Nodin was in Year One Decoction, was down the hall from Nodin's class. They reached the door at the same time as another group. Nodin found herself looking into the dark eyes of Ivor Daunte. Willow, Odette, and Ascelin all stopped, letting them go first.

Nodin kept walking, unaware of her friends dropping behind. "Nah ahh, wanna-be-nobody," a snarling voice drawled at her. Nodin felt the swell of the weave before she felt the grasp of magic wrapping around her.

Instinct had her pulling apart the magic before she could think, instead she let it hit her, and braced for the jolt to come. Nodin was thrown across the floor, her knees buckled as she skidded across the floor. "Know your place, weakling." Ivor smiled at her as he walked away. *My place? Yours is under my boot.*

Nodin stayed on the floor till they all left and her friends darted over to her. "Asshole," Nodin seethed, brushing herself off. "Be careful. They are powerful," Ascelin said, pulling Nodin to her feet. "Don't make them your enemy," Willow added.

6

Spending dinner by herself, Nodin powered through a plate of morchella mushroom pasta salad, and a plate of oyster mushroom risotto. Cleaning up her table, she kept her head down. Though the room was not staring and whispering about her, it sure felt like it. Needing some space, Nodin avoided going back to her dorm. Walking around the halls of the school, she matched up the doors she was strolling past with the rooms on her maps.

Over an hour later, Nodin was still walking around the halls, lost in her head. She came to a dead end, where a simple metal door stood slightly ajar. Gently brushing her fingers over the cool surface, it almost jumped out from under her fingers to swing open. The air that filtered through the door was deep and rich, earthy and clean. Slipping into the room, Nodin pushed the door back into place behind her, with the palm of her hand. Nodin found herself in a massive greenhouse filled to bursting with plants, and trees.

Unlike many greenhouses, this one was a massive enclosed garden, with paths winding through a forest of greens, peppered with bright splashes of flowers. Drifting between the huge leaves that hung low over the path, Nodin brushed her fingers over the foliage. Hundreds of plants that Nodin could name on sight, yet hundreds more she could not. So many she had never seen before.

In what felt like minutes to Nodin, but had been over an hour, Nodin came to a single glass door in the wall that opened up to outside. Nodin waved her fingers through the air, pulling at the weave, and the door popped open. Stepping out onto a thick blanket of grass, it swept over several sloped hills, rolling down towards a dark forest. A smile broke over Nodin's face. She had much missed the company of the trees. Nodin kicked off her shoes, whisking them off to her room before they hit the ground with a slight tug at the weave.

Nodin wiggled her toes in the grass, feeling the soft cool blades tickle at her ankles. Taking a few skipping steps, before breaking out into a run, she held her arms out wide, feeling the wind wrapping around her as she ate up the ground. Making it over three of the sloping rolls in the ground, she spun around and collapsed to the ground, looking up at the sky.

Sucking in deep breaths, digging her fingers into the ground, scratching into the earth, Nodin gently wrapped herself in the weave, tucking and tugging at it till it folded around her, and then she jumped from her place on the grass to the middle of the trees. Once again a wild animal.

Breathing in through her nose, filling it with the damp earth smell, her eyes filled with the mottled green of the forest floor. Nodin listened to the groaning of the trees and branches around her, the muted sounds of the small creatures moving about, and the soft bubble of a creek. Her fingernails were caked in dirt, the soles of her feet stained with soil, a deep part of her soul relaxing within her. The pieces of her soul settled back into place, clicking together, becoming whole once again.

Nodin followed the edge of the stream, dipping her fingers into the frosty water. The water pulsed through her fingers and down the stream. Nodin relished the bite of the rocks that built up the shallow bank. The cold edges of the rocks were not yet smoothed with time, much like her. Nodin had lost track of time: had she spent minutes or hours in the forest? Nodin did not mind. The creek rushed over a small cliff, before continuing along the forest. Nodin split from the stream and worked her way through the trees. Climbing over large boulders covered in moss, down a fallen tree, her fingers brushing several deep gash marks in its bark.

Nodin jumped down to the forest floor, and pushed an overgrown raspberry bush aside. Behind the raspberry bush, the forest opened up to a clearing, a pebbled beach dipping into a large lake. The light bounced off the surface of the lake, the rippled outlines of large boulders underneath.

Nodin walked up to the water's edge, dipping her toes in the clear water, ripples expanding from her skin. A large, twisted tree grew from between the rocks in the shore line. She settled at the foot of the tree, nestled between two large roots which looped up from under the rocks, growing thick with moss.

Nodin stayed snuggled up in the tree's roots till the sky started to dim, the sun settling beneath the blanket of the forest.

Closing her book, having been lost in its pages, Nodin looked around, the forest much darker in the dim glow of sunset. The dark twisting trees did not scare Nodin as she retraced her steps back home. Just as much a predator with teeth as anything else out here. *Watch out, we bite.*

Her bare feet soft and silent of the old stone Nodin crept through the abandoned halls of the school towards her beckoning bed. The whole school was plunged into a deep dark night. Tiptoeing past her shoes sitting on the floor by her bed, Nodin fell into bed. Scooping a loose blanket under her head, she wiggled beneath the covers. The dark room caressed her mind, settling over her like a thick blanket soothing her to sleep.

7

"Nodin!" The world swam around her, in a milky slurry. "Nodin!" Her whole body shook as Nodin blinked away the darkness pooling in her eyes. Ascelin's face peered down at her. A cold palm lightly tapped against her warm cheek. "Get up!" Ascelin hollered at her, tugging on her arm. "Class starts soon." Ascelin dragged her out of the bed, not commenting on her dark brown soles.

Throwing on her school uniform from the day before, tucking her books under her arm, and straightening her clothes, Nodin ran from her room. Joined by Ascelin in the living room, they ran from the dorm and straight to class. Their feet ate up the stone halls, skidding into class just before it started. Odette and Willow had saved two spaces for them in the middle of the classroom.

They sank into their seats as the Professor opened the textbook, flipping through a couple of pages before starting his lecture. Nodin flipped through her textbook to find the right page, trying to follow along with the professor. Something sharp jabbed into her ribs. Ascelin pulled her hand back from Nodin's side, her face still turned to her book. She discreetly pointed at Willow, whose hand was reached out under the desk. In her hand was a cookie.

Nodin slipped it from Willow's grasp, placing it on the desk picking chunks of it off, and sneaking them into her mouth. Spreading out her notebook, she reached for her pen, coming up empty. Frowning, she thought back to when she last had her pen. *Last night.* She had placed the pen down on the ground next to her book. The book! She had left it at the lake.

Twisting her fingers, the rest of the class Nodin's mind was at the lake with her book. It had been the last book her father had given her before… *before you killed him.* Her fingernails dug into her palms snapping herself out of her thoughts. "Ready?" Ascelin was standing up looking at her.

Nodin snatched up her books. "Yes." She followed behind them in silence. "I'm just gonna go grab something." She waved her hand over her shoulder vaguely towards the dorm. She turned and ran her tail tucked, before the others could protest, expertly slipping through the throng of people, disappearing in the crowd.

8

Nodin strutted down the hall to her dorm, slipping through the living room and into her dark escape. Between the step she took into her room and the next she jumped all the way to the lake. The weave folded around her, folding between the points. The weave unfolding around her, spitting her out. She marched over the stones to the tree. Nodin searched the base of the tree, looking under all the roots. Her book was missing. *It's gone.*

Huffing out a hot puff of air, Nodin leaned against the tree. Her hair sat in wisps around her head, escaping the braid she had wrestled it into. A small black and brown bird landed on the branch by her head. Letting out a little cheep at her, Nodin looked over at her new friend. Sitting right next to the bird was her book. The bird looked at her with small black eyes. Letting out a single cheep it jumped into the air and was gone with two flaps of its wings.

Nodin slipped the book from its place, resting on the branch leaning against the trunk. Her pen was clipped to the back leather of the book. A small corner of paper stuck out from between the pages. Gently prying the paper from the book she

39

looked at it, the shadow of writing on the other side. The tip of her finger wormed its way under the first fold, flicking it open. The short sharp script fanned along a diagonal on the paper.

Great choice of book. Don't want it to get ruined.

In place of a signature, there was a rough outline of a Wyvern, its tail looping around its body. One of the pages in her book was dog-eared, well many pages were, but this one was new. Letting the page fall open in her palms, along with the notes left by her father there was a passage underlined in darker ink.

For those who see the world, all is broken.

Nodin smiled down at the page, letting the weight of the words wash through her. Flipping the note over to the blank backside, Nodin scrawled her own message back. Using the well-known words in the sister book to the one in her hands. One many theorists suggested it was the second half of the proverb.

From shattered worlds come shattered people.

Signing the bottom of the quote with a swirling pointy ivy leaf and folding the note back up, Nodin tucked the note firmly in the nook of the tree where her book had been waiting. Slipping back through the weave to her dorm room, Nodin joined her friends for lunch. A new smile graced her face as the thoughts of the note-writer sank into her mind.

9

Nodin kept sneaking back to the lake, drawn to it for its peace, but secretly loving the connection she felt to her new pen pal. While her fellow classmates were fine company, they only wished to discuss what they were learning in class or anything but -not wishing to help her understand what she didn't understand. Her pen pal enjoyed the discussion of philosophy, some of the greatest and most controversial thinkers of their time, and many of the past.

All the letters she had received from her elusive pen pal sat in a drawer in her desk, bundled up together with a silky green ribbon. Each was written on scraps of paper, some large, some small, all different types of paper, her favorite was definitely the paper that seemed to be handmade. The rough thick paper was gray in color, small pieces of flowers and leaves pressed into each page.

Each night she slipped into bed with soil-stained soles, and a fresh letter to add to her bundle. Along with all her letters was a fresh pile of books for her to dive into recommended by her correspondent. She secretly hoped they had a matching pile that she had recommended. This night was no different.

Nodin returned from the lake aching and tired, a letter clutched to her chest, smiling at the ceiling. Rolling over her bed, she tugged out her little bundle of joy, slipping off the green ribbon, the gentle crinkle of the paper soothing. She gently placed her new one on the top of the others, thumbing through them.

Some nights she stayed up mulling over who the author could be. A million options ran around her head. Slipping the ribbon back around the bundle, setting it safely in the draw of her side table, Nodin settled in bed. Her mind did not race this night, and sleep welcomed her into its loving embrace.

10

Nodin walked from breakfast to class with Willow and Odette. Ascelin was still in bed, complaining that she was one-hundred percent dying. She had the stomach flu. Willow kept going on about something she had read in the next chapter of the textbook.

Nodin was so engrossed in what Willow was talking about, she didn't see the leg swing out in front of her. Someone slipped their foot right out in her path, hooking her ankles, pulling her legs out from under her. As Nodin slammed into the floor, her books went flying.

Pushing herself up, off the floor, laughter echoed through her spinning head. Her fingers had dug deeply into the weave on instinct, she uncurled her fingers leaving the weave as it had been. She looked up at the laughing faces above her. It was the heirs and their gaggling group that followed them around. Two of the young men were laughing and shoving at each other in congratulations.

As if they had just done the funniest thing in the world. Nodin gritted her teeth, tempted to retaliate, but schooled her anger as she collected her books from the floor and ran back over to Willow and Odette's horrified faces. "Are you okay?" Willow pulled her into a hug. Odette smoothed out her hair as best she could. "A little bruised but I will survive." Nodin looked over as the group, still laughing, walked away down the hall.

She slipped into her classroom, head down. Willow and Odette slipped into the only two seats available in the middle of the class, and Nodin waved at them before settling in the back.

"The most important tool in your tool box is?" the professor boomed. Several students raised their hands at the rhetorical question. "Shielding," the professor answered his own question. "Shielding is considered a form of raw magic, however, it is more a form of aspect-less magic." The professor droned on about the history and importance of shielding before he went into the mechanics of how to form a shield.

"And now you can practice!" Everyone stood up at his words and crumpled their faces in concentration, the weave rippled and bubbled all around the room -screaming in protest as the magic was ripped and torn into.

Nodin wrinkled her face in mock concentration, as she watched the class. There was a range of success. The professor walked around the room, handing out praises or advice to each student. By the time he reached Nodin, the weave was in shreds. She summoned a gentle ripple of raw magic in front of her. One of the worst shields in the class by far, however, not the complete bottom. Enough that the professor gave her some stern words of advice, but then moved on to another student.

Huffing out the breath she had been holding, she settled back into faking her way through the class. This may be harder than she had originally thought.

Nodin lost Willow and Odette in the crowd as they stormed out of the classroom, all discussing the shielding they could conjure and how they were going to practice. Nodin scuttled to the side wall, letting everyone behind her pass by. She settled her breathing, taking in several deep gulps of air. As the crowd dispersed the classroom opposite her opened up and more students flooded the hall.

The heirs piled out first, their ever present cloud of people following behind. Ivor's loud laughter filled the hall. Clovis and Roman were fooling around with each other pulling at each other's clothing, laughing as well. Nodin watched them sharply, taking in the group like circling sharks.

Sticking to the wall Nodin inched down the hall, adamant not to be left alone with them. Clovis swung the book in his hand at Roman, and the book connected with his chest. Staggering back, Roman clutched at his chest, smiling at his friend. Pulling a leather notebook from under his arm, Roman swung back, clipping Clovis's shoulder. Nodin froze, her eyes locked onto the notebook. It was stained a dark green except for the carved wyvern with its tail wrapped around its body.

The floor shattered from under her. Nodin turned and fled

down the hall. The weave reached out and brushed up against her, trying to sooth her thundering soul. He can't be. *Oh, yes, he can.*

~

Nodin ripped through her room, pulling the blankets from her bed, wrenching open the desk drawer. Wrestling the ribbon from around the letters, flipping through each letter. Checking, hoping that just one would prove her wrong, none did. She sank to the floor letting the letters go, panic wrapping its bony fingers around her heart.

Nodin refused to visit the lake for over a week. Instead, she spent the week making sure she placed in the lowest third of all her classes. Her skin sat tight on her, chafing and pinching, chapped. Even more than avoiding the lake, she avoided the heirs.

11

Nodin nuzzled deeper into her warm blankets, and rolled over to look out the window. It was many hours into the night, and Nodin was restless under the stars. Slipping out of bed, she put on a pair of leggings and a thick wool sweater. Tucking her wild hair into a loose bun she took a deep breath and looked out of the window. Between one blink and the next she was back at the lake. The lake sang back at her, deep blue reflecting the dark sky above. Nodin watched the lake; not a ripple on the surface, an endless pit of stars in the ground.

Two letters were tucked neatly in the crook of her tree, sitting there waiting for her. Nodin tugged the damp paper from the branch, and brushed off a little dirt. Careful not to rip the soft paper she unfolded the letters. She stared at the signature before reading anything else. The pit in her stomach opened its mouth and chewed on her.

Nodin spun and darted towards the lake pulling her arm back ready to throw them into the water. She froze at the edge. Her fingers dug into the paper crumpling it, waiting. Nodin's arm dropped to her side, letting the letter float to the ground. She looked out over the lake, watching the nightlight bugs dance over the surface, spinning with each other lighting up the night with their pale blues and greens.

Nodin scooped up the letters, flipping them open again. She took them in slowly. The first letter had continued their discussion of the politics in the poetic work of Zale Jareth. The second was one single line.

I miss you.

Nodin stared at the words. The simple little words did not fit in with the man she now knew wrote them. The short, sharp scrawl etched into the page looked back at her. Underneath his letter Nodin quickly jotted down two words.

Roman Van'Hight.

Nodin slipped the letter back in the crook of the tree, keeping the first one. Nodin turned her back on the tree and slipped into the water, a small bubble of air wrapping around her to keep her dry. Nodin walked along the bottom of the lake, till it bottomed out into a deep chasm carving into the earth. Nodin sat on the edge of the cliff, her legs dangling off the edge. She watched the creatures of the lake sleep around her.

Nodin surfaced over an hour later, dry as a summer's day. She gently splashed some cool water over her face, before walking back through the twisted trees, enjoying the darting shadows around her.

Little predator.

Nodin was almost out of the forest before she folded the weave around her, stepping into her room. Flopping into bed she slipped the new letter into the drawer, but didn't take the time to slip it under the ribbon. Nodin could not sleep. She tugged the book off her desk she flipped through the pages. Zale Jareth was a prolific poet in his time. Nodin sank into his familiar words. Zale painted a bloody image of the time before Elves had retreated from the world. The brutal truth painted in beautiful words.

12

Nodin left the lake alone the next night, catching the missing sleep she had not found the night before. When she returned to the lake the day after that, between classes, the letter was gone, but no response sat in its place. She crushed down the feelings clawing up her throat, and ground her teeth to keep her emotions at bay.

Nodin checked the lake sporadically between school life. Roman showed no outward signs that he had read the letter, and Nodin had watched the whole group vigilantly. Not a hair or cocky smile out of place.

Nodin stewed over her oatmeal, chasing the raisins around the bowl. Roman sat with his gaggle of admirers, he was waxing about some achievement Nodin was sure was handed to him on a silver plate. *Spoon sucking moron.* Nodin stabbed at her dish, watching the group. How did he even get to the lake? She had searched around the lake for any clue of how he managed to reach it.

Shy of animals, Nodin hadn't found any disturbances in the surrounding foliage. Nodin's spoon scraped the bottom of her bowl, empty, she quietly returned the plate. Leaving the dining hall in a foul mood, by the time she made it to her class she had shifted from anger to pain. She missed her pen pal deeply, the polar opposite of everything she knew about the Van'Hight heir. That version must be somewhere in that man, her version. *Her version.*

Nodin spent much of class with her mind at the lake. Deep at the bottom of the lake, floating down into the chasm the darkness swallowed her whole. *Into the darkness.*

<h1 style="text-align:center">13</h1>

Nodin ground her teeth as the professor bit into the class for their low academic scores. She disliked this professor to no end. Supposedly, they were learning about raw magic, how to use and not use it, in the first year's case, not use. She had spent hours in this class listening to this professor claim to be one of the most powerful raw magic users of their time.

Nodin glared out the window. The raw magic she loved so much was ripping the weave right out of the world. The soul of the was universe pulled apart and contorted into pretty little party tricks for this professor. Nodin would bet the skin on her back that in a fight she would ground her bones to dust before the professor could get their greasy fingers on the weave.

Nodin stormed out of the class right as the professor dismissed them, flying down the hall. She shoved past all the bodies, her shoulder slamming into a solid mass of muscle. She looked up into Ivor's cold eyes. "Watch it," Ivor growled. Nodin met his gaze, not backing down from him this time. "Oh bite me, little bug," Nodin snapped back at him, pushing past the group. *Show them your teeth.*

Everyone warned her not to cross the heirs, especially Ivor who had a mean temper and a control complex. They didn't even know the predator among them.

~

Nodin stumbled, her bare knees hitting the floor. The bite of the coldness of the stone worse than the bite of the stone ripping through her flesh. Pushing herself up, she pulled her leaden legs one step in front of the other. Running down the empty hall, the walls were bare gray stone, disappearing into an endless dark.

Not a window or a door to mark how far she had run. Her lungs burned, fighting against the air she so desperately needed. The corridor turned to the left sharply. Nodin ricocheted off the wall, her finger tips digging into the unforgiving stone. She gasped, her lungs void of air, and she stumbled fighting to stay on her feet. The rhythmic tap tap of claws echoed from down the hall she had just turned off.

Nodin pushed her legs harder, ignoring the burn in her muscles and ache in her joints. She whipped her head around trying to see what was behind her. The grinding sound of its claws on the stone grew louder.

Nodin's ankle buckled from under her, pitching her forward right into the stone beneath her. Her head connected with the solid stone. The world swam in a foggy ringing in her ears.

"Hello, little monster."

Nodin screamed, yanking the blankets from around her sweaty limbs. She panted into the night, sliding from the bed. A warm liquid dripped down her legs, swiping at her shins she brought her fingers up to her face. Blood smeared her finger tips. Pulling the nightgown up, she poked at her knees. The deep scrapes stung as she prodded at them. Padding quietly out of her room, she crossed the living room into the small bathroom.

Nodin dabbed at the broken skin, cleaning up the blood. She splashed her face with cold water and sneaked back to bed. Pulling her damp blankets off, she spread them out over the floor. Nodin sank into her bed, resting her hands on the sides of her face. Her ears picked up all the little noises of the walls around her.

$$14$$

Nodin wasted away over an hour in her bed. Nodin gave up on sleep, throwing off the remaining blankets she wrapped herself in a loose shawl. The gentle whisper of the weave on her skin was the only indication she had left her room.

The moon shone brightly, cutting a path through the darkness. A pool of liquid night, a twin of the moon sitting in dancing starlight. Nodin reached down into the stars, scooping up a handful of water, letting it slip through her fingers joining the constellations beneath. Dipping her toes in the cool water, she waded into the lake, up until it licked at her knees. She looked up at the sky, tracing the outline of her soul in the stars.

Nodin slowly drifted to shore, ending up spread out on the bank of the water, her fingers outstretched drifting through the sky. The longer Nodin spent among the stars the clearer her mind got. Her hand drifted to the shadowy outline of her tree, and she paused looking over its branches. No letter.

Nodin bit into her lip, feeling her pulse under her teeth. She tipped her head back letting the scream rip from her lungs -a warning. She sprung forward, the lithe speed of a predator, her feet dipped into the shallow water of the lake. The surface of the lake remained still, not a ripple as Nodin slipped below the surface. She clawed her way deeper and deeper into the lake.

Nodin grasped the beating heart of the lake digging in her fingers till she felt the lake shudder under her grip. Snarling at the abyss far beneath her. She let her pain free a beast even she could not tame. She let her pain free, deep into the darkness under the lake letting it eat her up. The darkness of the lake held her pain like a baby bird, flightless and ugly, taking it all in.

The darkness nurtured her pain till it grew up and grew wings of its own. Nodin sank deeper and deeper, the beast in her snapping and snarling. She let it go. Dark wafts of shadows darted from her body, darker than the light-less void she floated in. *Hello, little monster.* Nodin's eyes flashed open. She ripped her shadows from the world around her.

Nodin took a breath in -her lungs expanding with air miles under the surface of the lake. Something had heard her bark and now wanted her bite. Nodin brushed the dark water under her as a goodbye and a promise. She kicked upward, rising slowly through the water till her head broke the surface. The darkness watched her in silence, watching the venomous creature that was at home in its domain.

Nodin floated in the middle of the lake. Her hair fanned out around her as she watched the sky above -the world breathing peacefully around her. Nodin's shawl tugged at her shoulders, weighed her down, until it finally slipped off her shoulders and sank into the depths. Nodin was left in her sleepwear. Despite the cold, the ice around her heart grew colder -her soul remained a blaze with venom. She was the rose and the thorn. The darkness had taken a bite, and she had taken one right back smiling as the darkness ran from her in fear.

15

The warm light of the sun caressed her skin. Nodin blinked as the rising sun melted her cocoon of rage. It had wrapped her tight and kept her safe and warm -or so she had told herself. The sun peeked through the trees as the forest woke up around her. The rage felt colder and colder in her chest. She was a wounded animal.

Tears swelled in her eyes and dripped down her cheeks and dripping into the lake like little seeds, dropping from wilted roses, to bloom around her. She was more than rage and pain and venom -slowly her heart cracked in her chest, and the pain poured out of her.

The forest to her left stirred, the trees whispering, as something moved through it. Something not of the forest was shifting through the trees, its footsteps echoing in the roots of the wilderness. Nodin hung suspended in between her pain, unable to move, scared she would rip herself open on the jagged piece of her soul.

As footsteps reached her ears, Nodin glanced at the shore line, where a dark figure walked towards the beach. The tall figure looked out over the lake, observing her. Nodin watched as everything unfolded in front of her. Silently, the person broke into a run, flying over the ground in long strides.

Sliding in the rocks, coming to a stop as the lake kissed the toes of his shoes, Nodin smiled to herself as she watched Roman stand at the lake, panting. They watched each other for a heart beat, the world slowly as a whole life time passed in an instant. "Hey!" Roman's haunting voice called out to her.

To a stranger -she was nothing to him.

Yet.

"Get out!" She could hear the panic that gripped his chest. He stomped at the edge of the water, debating the risk of braving the water. *Little boy might drown.* "Get out! It's dangerous! Please!" Roman called, pulling his book bag off his shoulder and starting to shed his coat. Nodin dipped down into the water, swimming towards him without a word. She watched as he kicked his shoes off, letting the cold water soak into his socks.

"I'm perfectly safe," she answered as her toes gripped onto the stones of the base of the lake. She walked slowly towards him, curious if he would recognize the shy failing student within her. The wolf had shed its sheep costume. "How can I help you?" Nodin asked, coming toe to toe with Roman. She looked at him, taking in his endless eyes. Roman's face was flat, unreadable. Nodin didn't bulk from him, she watched his eyebrow twitch at her defiance.

This was not the behavior he expected. Nodin blinked slowly at him. Roman's lips twitched slightly as his mind struggled to piece together all the information before him. "Ivy?" Nodin froze, her eyes locked on his . "Roman," she purred, smiling at him. "How did you know?" Roman, swallowed nervously. "I guessed, looks like I guessed right." Nodin stepped back. "You signed your letters with the symbol on your notebook." Nodin waved her hand at his books, now spilling out of his book bag all over the ground.

Roman picked up the books from the ground. Nodin took her chance to take all of Roman in, his long limbs covered by simple but exquisite fabric. He really was a work of art, poetry in physical form.

"You have my name, can I have yours?"

"Nodin."

16

Roman grabbed his coat from the ground, offering the warm thick fabric to her. Nodin grasped the fabric, her fingers brushing against his. Slipping into the arms of the coat, it swamped her, consuming her. Nodin could smell the subtle scent of earthy musk and something floral she could not place. Nodin found herself getting lost in Roman's eyes again. Her finger brushed the sleeve of the coat absently. Roman's eyes drifted from her to his books in his arms. Nodin smiled at the titles he was holding, some of which he had recommended to her all those weeks ago.

"Have you read her later work?" Roman traced the top of a book. "Yes." Nodin smiled at him, she had devoured all her works after he had recommended them to her. "Did you know her cousin also wrote?" he asked, smiling back at her.

"I did not." Nodin smiled shyly at him. Roman's eyes flicked to the sunrise, and Nodin twisted to see the sky, a light with golden clouds. "Stunning," Roman breathed next to her. She glanced at Roman as his eyes slid back to the sky.

Roman and Nodin ended up sprawled out on the grass under the tree line -with their noses in books and their ankles touching. The gentle warmth that radiated from Roman, easing Nodin into a gentle lull. "I have class soon," Roman whispered. Nodin looked up from her page at him. Hope danced around his eyes. "Me too." Nodin sat up, looking down at her clothes.

"Keep it." Roman nodded at the book in her hands, one finger holding her place. Roman stood and brushed himself off. Nodin moved to pull the coat from her shoulders to return to him. "And that," he added. Nodin started to protest. "Return them when you are done reading the book." Roman smiled at her before turning and leaving through the trees.

Nodin sat still and waited till she lost track of his footsteps. She ran her fingers through her half-wet tangled hair. Dipping her nose down, Nodin took a deep breath. The deep earthy floral scent filled her nose once again.

17

It took Nodin over half an hour to get her appearance back to the humble school student, and she missed breakfast. Nodin floated through her classes, sketching the plants in her Herbology class into her note book, neglecting to write any notes on their properties. Nodin's mind kept pulling her to the lake, and the hours she had spent next to Roman reading.

The way his eyes had drifted over her, and the gentle way his hands flipped the page in his book. The lazy way his hand had rested on his forehead. The feel of his warm ankle against hers. The smell of him, waterlilies and musk.

Nodin left her class, her mind full of Roman instead of plants. Nodin had a mission -food. Her stomach was twisted in knots from her night spent awake, and missing breakfast. Nodin didn't make it to the dining hall before she ran into the heirs. Nodin looked them over about to open her mouth -Roman stepped forward, sliding his body in front of hers.

He turned towards his friends continuing his conversation, but his fingers ran down Nodin's wrist. His fingers disappeared before they reached her palm. Nodin stared at the wall of his back, the message clear, the crisp lines of his uniform frowning back at her. Nodin frowned at his back

As Roman and Ivor left the scent of waterlilies and musk met her nose. Making her stomach drop in a whole new way than at the lake. Nodin watched them walk away as if the hours they had shared were a dream. Nodin shook her head and marched herself to the dining hall, banishing Roman from her mind. Grabbing a plate of rich and spicy coconut curry and crispy fried rice, she ate it alone. Her mouth and soul on fire she returned to class with a renewed focus on her studies.

She left classes with studious notes, yet Nodin did not know what a single word meant. She had made a mistake, she was a sheep in wolf's clothing, she was here to fulfill a purpose and anything else was an unnecessary distraction. She had carved out a place for herself in this world, alone, and she would thrive. She needed to graduate from the school to move through the world and not have her casting questioned. Not have her life at risk for what she was. Not to be at risk for the blood in her veins. *Show your teeth, little predator.*

Willow, Odette, and Ascelin joined Nodin at dinner. Their bright bubbly conversation pulled her from the dark depths of her mind. Nodin picked at her sparse salad, as she caught up with her roommates. Ascelin made her promise that she would join her in her homemade face mask spa day that evening. Ascelin deemed that the mango mousse was to die for, as Ascelin floated back to the buffet table to get everyone a dessert.

Nodin's eyes settled on a familiar pair across the room. Roman spoke to his friends, in between bites of his food, but not once did his eyes leave hers. As Ascelin placed a plate in front of her, Nodin pulled her eyes from his, turning her back on him, and not looking back for the rest of her meal.

As their quartet left the dining hall, Nodin felt the heavy gaze of Roman track her across the room. Nodin held her head high, keeping her back to him. As she got farther down the hallway, the weight lifted from her and by the time she made it back to her dorm, she was excited for a quiet night with her roommates.

Many hours of giggling later, they all sat around the fire, their faces covered in all manner of sticky goo. Nodin had an oat and avocado mask dripping from her face. Ascelin had a honey and yogurt one. Odette opted for a green tea and honey mask while Willow had an oat and yogurt mask. A large chunk of Ascelin's mask fell from her face and hit the floor. All four women burst out into laughter, reducing them to tears. Nodin clutched her stomach as she fought to draw breath.

It was late when Nodin crawled into bed, collapsing into her blankets. Sleep found her quickly.

18

It was still dark out when Nodin's eyes fluttered open. Outside the window, the sky blushed pink. Something in the darkness kissed the edge of the sky, called to her -echoing deep from within the earth. Nodin followed the call -and stepped from her room to the forest. Nodin picked her way through the last couple of trees -the enchanting draw of the lake ebbing and flowing around her.

Nodin walked towards the lake, its haunting call pulling her forward. "I thought the lake was dangerous?" Roman flinched and spun to face her, his muscles wired -a spooked animal. "It is," Roman said, "so am I." Roman stared at her with a wolfish shit-eating grin on his face. Nodin glared at his face.

Every second she spent looking at his chiseled jaw her heart melted, and she fought her mind to keep her face twisted to a deadly point. "I'm sorry," Roman's grin only got wider as Nodin frowned deeper. "For?" Nodin snarled at him. Roman's jaw twitched as he weighed his words. Roman finally settled on his words. "The other heirs can't know we are friends."

"Friends?" Nodin's heart fluttered, beating against its cage in

66

her chest. "Yes," Roman confirmed. Nodin's heart started to splinter in her chest. *Only friends...* Why did she want more? Since when did she want more? "Why can't they know?" Nodin's mouth formed the words before her mind stopped her. Roman let out a sigh, tipping his head back. "It's a political minefield that impacts the future ruling body of millions." Roman stepped back, his body collapsing from the weight of his responsibility.

"And they are sharks that will eat you alive." Nodin softened her face at the young man before her, broken down by time he hadn't even lived yet. "So, at school we don't know each other, but here we are ... friends?" A small sadness danced in the back of his eyes. "Yes." The last piece of Nodin's heart shattered in her chest. "Okay." Nodin plastered on a smile, hiding her own sadness deep in her eyes.

Nodin drifted through her class with a new spark in her wings. The gentle rhythm of her days and nights left her in a state of demure delight. Spending dinner with her roommates dissecting that day's lessons. Settling into a deep sleep, before rushing off to the lake in the early hours of the morning.

19

Nodin found herself alone in a back hall that she swore was not there a week ago, that led around the school and up towards dorm rooms. Nodin drifted through it, wrestling the man she saw at school and the man she spent every morning with. Nodin stopped in front of a black iron framed mirror, the tarnish of the silver peeking through around the edges.

As Nodin started to turn away from the mirror, something dark shifted deep within the glass of the mirror. Nodin's head whipped back, and an open maw of twisted yellow teeth dripping tar greeted her. Gasping Nodin stepped back, not breaking eye contact as the mouth closed.

The red eyes sunk deep into burnt flesh and blinked back at her. The amorphous shape of its head, shifted as if it didn't quite know what shape it wanted to be yet. It tilted its head looking back at her, slowly its burnt black skin turned liquid -shiny and soft looking.

Nodin stepped forward, reaching out her hand towards the glass. Just as Nodin's fingers hit the cold surface of the mirror the creature was gone from within. Nodin stared into it,

68

searching for a sign of the creature. Nothing. *Fool.* Nodin backed away, spun around, and marched back to her dorm.

By the time she stumbled into the warm living room her legs burned. The nights of the past week had been getting colder and colder. The bite of winter digging in its fangs. All the other girls in her dorm had retired to their rooms, drowning under a sea of homework.

Lighting a candle, Nodin curled up in its warm light and started to tackle her monsoon of homework. Nodin watched the night, relishing in its velvet touch. A single flake of pure white drifted past her window. Then another and another.

Large fat blobs of snow gently waltzed from the sky to the ground. Nodin watched as her black wonderland turned to a white abyss. The ground would be covered in a blanket by morning. Blowing out her candle, Nodin settled in bed, content to watch the snow fall outside her window.

Nodin blinked at the darkness blurring around her. The snow still drifted in a complex dance with the wind past her window. Nodin choked out a breath, her lungs fighting the mucus that coated her throat. She coughed, clearing her lungs, the air coming out of her mouth blooming in a white fog. Nodin froze, the long blackened finger ending in a sharp claw, clinging to the end of her bed.

It flexed its fingers, the skin cracking at the seams, bright red shining through the crack, leaking on to the skin around it. Blood dripped from its skin, then absorbed back into the skin as it sealed shut again. Nodin was frozen in bed, heart hammering in her chest, her mind going fuzzy. She was locked inside her own body, swimming and drowning in her head.

The black head of the beast rose from behind the bed, resting on its hands. While its hands looked rather mortal from the wrist to what could only be called its elbow, it was more like the limbs of a bird. Its long arms pulled its body up onto the end of her bed. Its skin fell off its body in large flakes leaving behind bright red raw patches of skin.

It crouched on legs that had the bones of raptor, but the look of an ape. Shifting its weight forward, it slowly started to move up the bed on all fours. Crawling toward her, its eyes closed, its head merely a skull with skin stretched over it. Giving it a bobble head look, unlike how it had appeared in the mirror.

One hand wrapped around her ankle, lumbering up her body. How the seven-foot creature managed to fold itself up and sit on her chest was impossible. Nodin stared where its eyes had been, frozen her lungs screaming for air. While it had folded its body to sit on her chest, it still weighed more than it looked like it should.

Lifting one long finger, it took her in with an eyeless stare -its head tilted like it was deep in thought. The tip of its claw grazed Nodin's lip. Nodin's jaw ached as the muscles clamped down, her teeth protesting the pressure. It pressed its claw harder into Nodin's lip, drawing blood. Nodin didn't flinch at the sharp bite of the pain, the blood pooling on her lips and dripping down her cheek. Slowly, blood began to seep through her lips, filling her mouth. Nodin fought for air, the warm liquid filling her mouth with copper.

Gagging, on her own blood, Nodin spluttered -spraying blood all over the dripping maw of the creature. Taking advantage of her open lips, it slipped its finger into her mouth. Her blood coated its finger, an acrid burnt taste mixing with the copper. It pushed its finger deeper and deeper into her mouth, the tip of its claw slicing down the back of her throat. Nodin coughed on the blood sliding down her throat, and choked on the horrific digit -unable to fight back.

As the last knuckle kissed her lips, the creature's entire finger sat in her mouth and throat. It opened its eyes, looking at her with solid black eyes. It blinked once. Nodin watched in silent abhorrence as the skin on its hand went smooth, turning to an oily black smudge. Nodin choked out a scream as she felt the oily black substance sliding off the creature's finger and down her throat. The putrid tar coated her mouth and throat -burning. The creature's skin slipped down her throat and into her stomach burning, scorching from within.

The beast pried her lips apart with another sticky finger. It opened its mouth, the gruesome yellow teeth snarling in her face. Sliding the remaining fingers past her lips, the shiny oil seeped up its arm as slowly the whole arm turned to thick oily tar. The creature forced its whole arm down her throat.Its liquid form slid down her throat slowly. Nodin's eyes bugged out as she fought to regain control of her body -to fight against the creature trying to force its way into her. Desperate to force her jaw close - to stop the beast from eating her alive from the inside out.

Nodin was desperate to fight back as the creature forced more and more of its liquid body down her throat. Over half the creature now burned through her stomach. Nodin gagged as she watched her skin burn, blistering and bubbling before her eyes. The pain seared across every nerve in her body as the last of the creature slid down her mouth. The last of the sticky tar coated her throat so thickly it closed off her airway. Nodin clawed at her neck begging for air, her blistered skin turning from dark red to black. Burning her from the inside. Nodin choked on the tar in her lungs.

Nodin gasped, clawing at her throat. No longer burning, no monstrosity in sight Nodin choked for air in her silent room. She ran her hands over her mouth, over her hands, and finally to her throat. Not a scratch. Nodin coughed, spitting a mouthful of blood into her hand.

Slowly, Nodin calmed down, banishing the nightmare from her body. She stayed in bed, curled up in a small ball under her covers, till the sun started to peek through the falling snow.

The dim gray glow of the night faded to a pale orange glow. Nodin bushed her finger tips over her neck one last time before locking away the fear that had gripped her mind for the last agonizing hours of the night. Stiffly, Nodin pulled her sore body from her bed, dressing warmly in many layers as she braced herself for the day to come.

20

Nodin did not share her classmates' excitement over the snow that morning, dragging her outer husk around the school. Her mind had been unplugged and dumped into a vat of molten glass. Her body was stiff and sore from the night before -a spectacular headache blooming in her jaw and up her skull. Fighting through the fog in her mind to get through the cacophony of bodies in the halls, Nodin was batted around by the waves of people. She came to a stop in the ocean of people by slamming into a rock -or a person. Ivor. His large hand gripped the back of her shirt, dragging her in a circle away from him.

"How many times do I have to tell you to watch where you are going or are you that slow?" Ivor growled in her ear. "Sorry," Nodin mumbled trying to pull the fabric from his grip. "How did you even get in this school?" Vane added, smiling at her like a ghoul. "I earned it," Nodin gritted, still trying to work herself free from Ivor's vice grip. "How do you earn a charity case?" Remus asked, looping his arm over Vane.

Nodin blocked out the snickering jabs they kept throwing her way. Laughing at their prey as they poked and prodded, trying to make it scream. The crowd had thinned out substantially, enough that Nodin could move around more freely. Her eyes landed on a familiar pair, and for a moment she was lost in their depth. Roman leaned against the wall, his body giving off an air of nonchalance -his face an unreadable mask. He watched the scene in front of him, not moving to spare her from his friends.

Nodin gritted her teeth, breaking eye contact with him. *Cumbubble.* Nodin twisted out of Ivor's grip, smiling sweetly at him. "Wouldn't want to waste more of your time."" Her voice dripped with honey and spite. She turned and marched away from the group of boys. *A bunch of thundercunts!* Nodin twisted her hair in her fingers viciously, her jaw aching from grinding her teeth. Nodin stormed through the school, a whirlwind of anger and indignation.

Nodin burned as she dumped her school bag on the floor of her room. She was a wildfire and everything was fuel to burn. She ripped her hair free of its ribbon letting it fan out in a wild mess down her back. Nodin jumped deeper into the forest than she ever had, miles past the lake. Her boots crunched on the frost-covered leaves.

The trees were so thick it was dark as night, the tree branches had caught all the snow creating a ceiling of ice. Nodin let loose, running through the silent forest, her muscles burning with every step she took. Tilting her head back, Nodin screamed into the frozen air till her lungs and throat burned raw. Nodin was a wild animal burning in the cold wonderland around her. The forest was asleep, under its blanket of snow. Nodin ran and ran her wild cries and calls turning from raw shrieks of anguish to loud whoops and calls of kulning calling the wilds to her.

Nodin walked her way to the lake, her cheeks flushed from the cold. Nodin's wild soul had settled among the branches of the trees she passed. Nodin jumped randomly through her walk towards the lake bringing her to the hidden wonders of the forest. By the time her frost-touched boots found themselves sliding over the icy stones of the beach, Nodin's fingers were red and numb.

The water danced definitely against the cold, refusing to freeze over. Nodin stepped lightly, walking along the top of the water, letting it lick the snow from her toes. Despite the sub-freezing temperatures, Nodin settled down on the surface of the water, splaying her fingers and feeling the heartbeat of the lake.

Nodin closed her eyes and opened her soul to the world around her. Listening to the forest breath, the gentle rhythm of the lake's heart, and whispers of the wind. Nodin's eyes did not open till the sky started to dim as the sun gave up its fight with the snow clouds.

Nodin made her way to shore, warmed from deep in her soul. Nodin stuffed her toes into the small stones of the beach, tracing the outlines of some simple ivy leaves. "There you are." Roman's panting voice huffed from behind her. He was just emerging from the tree line at a run. He was bundled up against the cold in a thick coat, a long scarf wrapped around his neck.

His hair was wildly windswept sprinkled with snowflakes. His clothes were askew as if he had dressed as he ran to meet her. His nose was bright red from the crisp air. His deep eyes shone brightly with panic as he sucked in lungfuls of the frozen air. He waited, just looking at her. Nodin bubbled with rage. *Now he's worried? Now!* In her mind's eye, the image of his unconcerned blank face flashed before her. Nothing like the young man panting before her. The fire she had thought she had extinguished burned to life in her, hotter than ever.

"How… How could you?" Nodin snarled at him, stumbling over her words as rage choked her. She was an injured animal biting back, lashing out with everything she had. Roman's face twisted in what could have been mistaken as pain but Nodin knew it wasn't -he was affronted by his actions. "Do you know how much it hurts to watch and not be able to stop it?" he yelled back. "Seeing you in pain," he whispered, not looking at her. *Not able to stop it? Not able? He chose not to.*

"Imagine how I felt? How I felt going through it," Nodin snarled, she burned and there was no stopping it. It consumed her. "What do you want from me?" Roman looked at her his eyes ablaze with an inferno too. "You know it can't be we there," he snarled. "We?" Nodin's fire gutted dying down in her chest. "Yes," Roman breathed, panting as he stepped towards her. His cold fingers grazed across her burning cheeks, and the wool of his fingerless gloves tickled her ear.

"We," he repeated, looking at her. His fingers rested on her jaw, his thumb almost brushing her lips. The cold pad of his thumb brushed the edge of her lip. Nodin watched a thousand emotions dance through his eyes. Roman dropped his hand and stepped back, the thundering of her heart beat bursting to life in her ears. Nodin turned her head away to hide the burning in her cheeks and the wanting in her eyes.

Nodin startled a little at the sharp sound of Roman's shoes on the rocks. He pulled her close, his hot breath fanning over her face. His searing hot lips met hers with the greed of a drowning man.

Roman's fingers rested lightly behind her ears, his fingers tangled in her hair. Nodin tugged at the front of his shirt through his open jacket. She pressed her body into his relishing the warmth. "Nodin," he whispered against her lips.

21

Nodin found herself in a dead world. Everything was gray and ashy, crumbling under her touch. The air was stale and stagnant in her lungs. Nodin reached out to the weave, but it broke in her fingers like cobwebs. A shadow of itself. What was going on? She ran down hall after hall looking for another living thing, a plant, a person, an animal, anything.

Nothing but gray walls greeted her. She came to an open room filled with massive windows, stretching up the vaulted ceilings. Outside was nothing but swirling gray dust. A brewing sandstorm of dust folding in on itself. Strong sticky fingers wrapped around her ankle. Nodin jumped, pulling at her leg to free herself. She turned to face her foe, the familiar burnt face looking back at her.

The fingers on her ankle turned to acrid tar spreading over her foot. The tar spread up the creature's arm, pulling her closer to its body. Slowly the liquid form of the creature encapsulated her leg, creeping past her knee. Nodin was frozen in place and she watched in horror as more of the creature disappeared into sludge, more of her body was covered in a thick layer of tar.

As the tar climbed up her diaphragm, Nodin found her voice, screaming at the top of her lungs. At the sound of her hoarse screaming, the creature picked up speed climbing up to her neck and choking her. It tightened around her, cutting off her air supply. Nodin's final breath died in a strangled scream.

Nodin choked on a strangled scream as she kicked at her blankets. The skin on her ankle was red and raw, almost blistered. Her nightmares were getting worse. Again.

22

Nodin stared blankly into her bowl of fruit topped with almond granola. Ascelin brushed her hair out of her face, pulling Nodin's wild hair into a bun and wrapping it with a scarf. Despite curling up in bed each night, she hadn't gotten a wink of sleep in three days. Her friends had gotten worried about her after night two, whispering behind her back. Nodin stared at the almonds on the top of her food numbly, every time she blinked the red eyes of the creature stared back at her from the darkness in her mind.

Her body was sore from the lack of sleep and her mind had long since stopped processing the world around her. Soon, she would start hallucinating -which she was sure would only bring more of the creature with it. She felt its claws brushing up against her mind, tracing over her crumbling walls.

She managed to eat a couple of bites of her breakfast in between chugging three cups of black coffee. As Nodin shuffled behind her friends towards her first class, she glanced over at Roman to see him watching her.

His eyes tracked her through the room as he continued to

converse with his friends. Nodin's head spun -unrelated to her lack of sleep. He disappeared, replaced by a solid wall of gray stone.

~

Nodin stood knee-deep in the freezing lake -fighting her sleep-sodden mind. The sky had cleared up from its dump of snow -letting the star shine through. The freezing lake woke up her blood, pulling her from the hallucinogenic fog she had been in all day. Out here under the stars, she was free from the grasp of the creature. *For now.* "Beautiful," a familiar voice said from behind her.

Roman stood there with his hands in his pockets looking at her before looking up at the sky. A smile painted his face as he walked closer to her. "What are you doing here?" Nodin's heart faulted in her chest as he stopped beside her, his shoulder brushing against hers. "Needed a study break." He shrugged, and looked out over the lake, refusing to look at her.

"You?" Nodin took a deep breath, it ratted down her throat. "Can't sleep," she whispered. "For how long?" His voice no louder than hers, like they were discussing a secret, keeping it from the world around them. "Three days," Nodin finally admitted after she let the silence drag on too long.

"Why?" Roman didn't look at her through the whole conversation. "Nightmares." It seemed like such a tame word compared to the torture her mind had put her through these past days.

"Come with me." Roman turned to her, grabbing her hand, and pulled her through the trees. She stumbled to keep up with him over the rough ground. Roman kept up his pace as they approached the castle, pulling her through the front doors by her hand -which was warmly tucked into his.

They quietly snuck through halls Nodin had never seen, passing dorm room doors till they were on the far, opposite, side of the castle from her dorms. This side of the castle was mirrored image to her side. "I thought there was no *'we'* in school," Nodin held up their joined hands. Roman looked at her over their intertwined fingers. "There is. Here we are." He stopped outside a dorm room at the end of the hall. Some doors down the loud voices of people filtered - a party raging behind its door.

"I trust them." He pointed to the door of his dorm room. "I thought you called them sharks." Nodin stepped back from the door. The thought of Ivor's sneering face as she battled through her sleepless night haunted by her nightmares, twisted her stomach. Nodin almost wished to face the creature again, rather than face Ivor.

"My roommates are not the other heirs," Roman said, smiling at her. "Oh, I would have thought they were," Nodin stumbled over her tongue. Roman didn't bother knocking on the door, instead opting to push the door open with his booted foot. "Honey! I am home!" he called into the space in a sing-song tone. Roman marched into a matching living room to hers, though decorated differently, pulling Nodin in with him.

Three unfamiliar men sat around a table playing cards, and they all looked at her with the same shit-eating grin plastered on their faces. "Oh who is this fine flower?" the speaker stood up and then vaulted over the back of the couch walking towards her. "Nodin," she introduced herself. "A pleasure." He gave her a shallow mock bow, taking her hand and giving it a light kiss. "Lockett, but everyone calls me Lock. And if I may be so bold I think I have found my key," he said, placing his hand flat on his chest winking at her.

"That is Sullen and that pisswizard is Kyrin," Lockett introduced the remaining two as they abandoned their game and came over to greet her. "Pisswizard?" Kyrin screeched at Lock, punching his friend in the arm. "Stop flirting, Lock," Sullen chided.

Nodin watched as Roman slowly started to relax, she watched the stress shed off his shoulders as he and his roommates joked around. Turning from a stressed young man to a carefree boy before her eyes. Nodin couldn't help but smile at their antics. The large fire in the hearth fought away the cold, keeping it at bay outside the stone walls of the room.

Sullen tried to rope Roman into their card game, claiming they needed him to keep Lock's cheating in check. Roman dodged the goading from his friends as he guided Nodin to his room. Stepping into the dark space, Nodin looked around; making out odd lumpy shapes of furniture through the gloom.

Flicking on the light behind her, Roman stood in the open door and watched her. Nodin scanned the room, breathing in the essence of the room. If one could paint Roman's soul this room was it. While stuffed to the brim with clutter; yet, it did not feel messy or overwhelming. Floor-to-ceiling bookshelves took over one wall, books bursting from the shelf. Trinkets decorated the bookshelf, a small tree carved from a dark green stone stood out to Nodin. It was an accurate tree of life. The tree stood as a symbol of rebirth in elven history. Most mortal depictions were twisted misrepresentations.

Roman's closet was only half full, sporting mainly school uniforms, a few comfortable clothing options, and several formal suits, all hanging in color coordination. His desk was full of notebooks and papers, all of which were sorted neatly except for the stack of papers he was clearly in the middle of working on, pens scattered across the paper. His window sill was filled with potted plants, growing wildly against the glass. The space was full to the brim of Roman, almost on the verge of messy.

Nodin found the room soft and warm. "Sorry about the mess." Roman swept the homework off his desk into his book bag. Nodin didn't think she had seen Roman so awkward. She was so used to the confident, high achieving student, or the full of talent wielder. Not the unsure boy that stood before her now.

"So we are just gonna…" Nodin started, her eyes drifting to his bed. "Yeah, but it's not like that…" He trailed off too, looking at his bed. Wordlessly they retreated to opposite sides of the room, Nodin facing his bookshelf and Roman at his closet. Taking a deep breath, Nodin started to pull her school uniform off. Her body protested - sore muscles pinching as she tugged off her clothes -leaving her in a soft pair of shorts, and her thin undershirt. Nodin waited, her eyes closed, fingers lightly running over her arm, for a clue Roman had changed.

"Nodin," he whispered. Slowly, she turned her head pounding, her vision swimming. Roman stood before her a god disguised in a man's body. His lean body was wrapped in muscles, his chest bare, loose gray pants sitting low on his strong hips. His wide eyes hid under his dark espresso hair - a wild animal that had been caught about to bolt.

Roman gently pulled at Nodin's elbows, guiding her to his bed. Letting her sit down on the side of it, she lay down on her side, facing the large window. Roman pulled the large puffy duvet over her, tucking the thick feather blanket around her. Roman crawled into bed behind her, settling down, taking care to not touch her. Nodin wiggled her legs gently, slipping one leg outside of the blanket, and hooking it around. Nodin listened to Roman breathe in the dark, for the first time all day, she felt wide awake.

Slowly, her wishes for sleep slipped from her fingers for another night. Roman turned over to face her, his warm breath fanning over her cheek. A heavy arm slipped over her hip, resting on top of the blanket. The weight over her body calmed her down, the warmth of his limb soaking through the fabric.

Slowly, Nodin's eyes fluttered shut in the warmth, as her mind drifted in the darkness Nodin felt the arm around her waist tighten and pull her across the bed till her back met a warm wall. Tucked in Roman's arms, Nodin fell asleep.

23

Nodin woke as the wall she was leaning against shifted. Nodin blinked at the deep pink sky that shone through the window. The wall behind her had been warm, and now her back felt cold in its absence. Nodin watched the sun rise in post-sleep bliss; her mind still waking up with the world around her. Her warm wall came back several heart beats later. Roman tugged her close to his chest, watching the sun rise over her shoulder.

"Morning mea nox lux," Roman mumbled, his voice thick with sleep. Nodin's skin flushed to the same shade of pink as the sky. "Morning," Nodin whispered back. "How'd you sleep?" Roman pulled his arm from around her, propping himself up on it -looking down at her. "Amazingly." Nodin smiled, closing her eyes. Roman's hair was tousled and hung in his face.

Roman pulled himself from bed, scooping up the pile of clothes she had left on his floor, and setting them on the covers before her. He grabbed a school uniform from his closet and wordlessly left for the bathroom. Nodin quickly dressed herself in yesterday's uniform. Twisting her matted hair into a crown around the back of her head.

Nodin rubbed her hands over her face. "Mea nox lux?" Roman stood at his bedroom door leaning against the door jam. "Meus rex tenebris," Nodin smiled at him. Nodin met him in the doorway, tilting her shoulders to slip by him. "Wait." Roman stopped her with two of his fingers against her wrist.

Nodin looked up at him, worrying her lip between her teeth. "Have a good day," Roman bid her farewell. "You too."

~

Nodin slipped into the empty chair beside Odette. "Where were you last night?" Ascelin asked, smiling at her over her plate of eggs. "You didn't come home," Odette added as she swirled her spoon in her bowl of congee. "Slept in another person's dorm," Nodin said as she nibbled on her toast. "Nodin!" Willow squealed. "Not like that!" The whole table burst out in laughter at Nodin's bright red face. Nodin was lost in class having spent the last couple of days in an insomniac stupor, and now she could not drag her attention from this morning's snuggle session.

Leaving her class with a smile on her face, and not a single word in her notebook, she had missed every time the professor had called on her, unable to answer a single question. In the hour they had been given to produce ten successful night lights, she had not made a single one. Despite her academic failure she had not had a happier day since she arrived at this rotten school.

As the girls sat down for lunch, Odette slipped a copy of her notes across the table towards Nodin without a word. Nodin swiped them into her bag sheepishly. "Are you going to tell us who has you in this daydream?" Willow leaned over the table smiling at her. "Nope." Nodin leaned back in her chair, fighting the urge to look over at Roman. She could hear his usual group of followers milling around boosting Ivor's ego.

Nodin did marginally better in the rest of her classes for the day, at least making it out of the classes with notes to study later but not a drop of information in her mind.

Nodin sat with Ascelin for dinner, Odette and Willow having made plans with other friends. Ascelin tucked into a large plate of moose stew, a heaping pile of fresh steaming hot cornbread being dipped into it. Nodin spoke between mouthfuls of miso, tofu, and seaweed soup. Her plate of spicy cucumber salad, Kimchi, and sesame-roasted edamame was waiting patiently for her. Nodin's eyes kept flicking to Roman's table. She watched out the corner of her as the heirs joked around with each other, Ivor throwing food at anyone who walked past their table.

Roman's eyes kept finding hers. Roman gave her a minuscule smirk, his finger suggestively rubbing the spine of the book she had lent him. Ascelin and Nodin dug into large bowls of toasted coconut ice cream laughing at an overconfident first-year who had tried to approach the heirs and had gotten rejected and had a bowl of spicy prawn soup thrown at him. *Serves him right.* "He is such a pompous dick in class," Ascelin snickered through her ice cream.

After leaving Ascelin with her homework in the common room, Nodin retreated to her dorm. Shedding her school uniform, she slipped on thick black pants, a long sleeve shirt, and a warm knitted shawl. Shoving on her boots, and picking up her book bag Nodin stepped to the woods around the edge of the lake. Nodin glanced around to check that Roman had not seen her.

Nodin worked her way to the lake, finding herself alone with the waves she settled down with her book. She read through the socio-political poetry of Melo Silex. It was well past dinner when the rustle of leaves met her ears. Lifting her eyes from her book, Roman stumbled from the foliage, his own books tucked under his arm.

"Finally," he breathed as he folded his body next to hers. He leaned his head against her shoulder. "I've been waiting for this all day." Roman slipped his arms around her waist, reading the page of her book over her shoulder. "Mea nox lux," Roman whispered under his breath, and Nodin flipped the page wondering if she was meant to hear his words; they had been so quiet. *My Night Light.*

"Can I sleep with you tonight?" Nodin did not look up from her page. "Can I sleep in your bed? I mean." Nodin stumbled over her words, shying away from the implication. "You are always welcome." Roman slipped his fingers into her hair, massaging her scalp. Roman started to recite a long waxing poem by Prue Debura, that lamented the journey of the moon. Nodin tilted her head back, listening to Roman's quiet words as he continued to massage her scalp, pulling the tangles from her hair.

24

After leaving Roman at the front doors of the school, she ran to her room, stuffing her book bag with clothes for her overnight stay with Roman. It wasn't long after nightfall that she found herself in front of his dorm door, another party pounding the walls down the hall. She rapped her knuckles against the worn wood of the door in two short sharp knocks.

"Come in," Lock swung the door open with a flourish, waving her into the dorm with a huge smile. As Nodin entered, Lock gave her a mock bow. Nodin laughed as she dipped into a curtsy. "Toadstool!" Lock called at the top of his lungs. Aloud clatter filled the air from the direction of Roman's room. He laughed at her frowning face. "He spends so much time reading that toadstools could grow on his shoulders." Lock left her by the door as the sounds of Romans footsteps joined the air.

"Mea nox lux," Roman purred, Nodin looked up at him. He was leaning against the door frame, eating her up with his eyes. Nodin blushed, her hands twisting around the strap of her bag. "Meus rex tenebris," Nodin greeted, walking towards him. She breezed past him and into his room. His room showed no sign of the crashing sound she had heard only moments earlier.

"You can sleep whenever you like, I unfortunately, have home-work due tomorrow." Roman shuffled towards his desk. It was in a state of disarray, papers and pens covered the table, books piled up on the corners. "I'm behind in mine too." Nodin joined Roman in his studies. Setting herself up on his bed, spreading out her books and notes.

Nodin worked through all her missed work, reviewing her notes from class. Nodin finished up the final touches of a paper on the effects of the root of the Milkworm plant. She looked up from her page, Roman was hunched over his paper, smudges of ink all over his hands. The room was lit by candle light, it flickered and bobbed all over the walls. "How is my excrucior artifex?" Nodin asked into the warm darkness.

Roman laughed softly. "Tortured artist?" Roman looked over at her, his eyes heavy with sleep. Nodin got up and ran her fingers through his hair, ruffling it up as she placed a single small kiss to his forehead. The moon was high in the sky, shedding light over the world, creating shadows that danced in the night.

Nodin wondered in the quiet bubble of night that they existed in -what they were to each other. He was the words to which her heart beat too, he was the silk that wrapped her soul, but he was also the son of the society who's hands choked the life from her. When she looked at him, the shadow of night resting on his face, hands smudged with ink -his lips reciting poetry, it was easy to forget who he was. Who he would become. Nodin's heart ached each day that she was reminded that one day soon it would be his hands choking her soul.

"It's late," Nodin whispered, pulling her fingers from his hair. How had she forgotten the power he held -especially over her? Nodin let his warmth be a balm to her soul, knowing the morning would hurt worse. The night wrapped them in warmth, protecting them from the world she lived in. Nodin fell asleep burning with pain in her bones.

For now, she would let him take up the space between the broken pieces of her soul. She would take every breath, every heartbeat, every moment with him the weave gave her, till his fingers would crush her -knowing one day he would be the death of her. Nodin drowned in a sleep so thick, so deep, that she had to fight to bring herself back to her body. It had only been a few hours, the night sky still an all-consuming void spanning out before her.

Nodin soaked in Roman's earthy water lily scent. Roman reached out of her in his sleep, wrapping his hand around her wrist -pulling her hand to his face and tucking it under his chin. Nodin smiled at the boy sleeping beside her. "Can't sleep?" the gravel of his voice scraped against the quiet night. "I got some good sleep." Roman pulled her wrist from under his chin, kissing along the veins of her wrist stopping at the palm of her hand. "My mind is lost somewhere in the possibilities of the future," Nodin confessed.

"Come back to me," Roman begged. Maybe he knew they were destined for catastrophe. "Stay with me." Nodin tilted her head back as Roman's lips crawled up her neck. "Here with you now, I will never leave," Nodin breathed as his teeth nibbled at the shell of her ear. "Stunning." Roman's eyes sparkled with reverence for her.

His hands cupped her face, as he took her soul in and worshiped her. Nodin felt as vast as the sky, his eyes staring into her; she felt like a goddess on earth. His worship fueling her divinity.

His lips crashed into hers. Consuming her, a drowned man gulping down water, taking her tongue in between his teeth. They fought, not each other, but side by side against drowning.

Roman lifted her, folding her up on his lap. She straddled his hips, rocking up against him. Roman grasped her waist, his fingers biting into her flesh, pinning her to him. Nodin bit down on Roman's bottom lip. Roman moaned into her mouth, his whole body reacting to her. Roman's hands tangled in her hair, pulled her head back allowing himself better access to her mouth.

Roman's tongue explored her mouth, his body weight pressing against her. Cradled in his lap, his hands in her hair, Nodin ground her hips into his. She watched as she drove him wild behind his dark eyes. Nodin grinned at him, their matching breath panting into the room.

Roman slipped his fingers into the waistband of her shorts, his fingers brushing softly against her skin. Roman pulled her shorts down, till they wrapped loosely around her ankles.

Nodin took a deep breath, looking at Roman kneeling before her. She was spread out on his bed, her knees in the air, feet planted together and hands behind her -holding herself up. Roman reached over, his finger brushing the delicate fabric of her panties along her thigh. His thumb brushed the damp fabric cupping her pussy. Nodin's legs shook slightly as his finger pressed into her warm core.

He sat back admiring her, wet and needy before him. "Take them off," Roman whispered. Nodin hooked her index fingers into the silk fabric, pulling them off of her hips, and down her legs till it was resting on her ankles with her shorts. Roman rubbed his hands up her legs over her knees and down her thighs -stopping at her hips. Roman took his time drinking her in, his eyes locked on her core. The sweet pink folds of her pussy bare to the air. Heating beneath his gaze Nodin started to squirm. Roman pushed down on her hips to stop her from moving. "Meum dulce exitium," Roman whispered to himself. Nodin's heart pounded in her pussy, her core tightening, each moment dampening her cunt. Roman leaned forward, taking his weight on his arms, dipping lower till he was inches from her pussy.

She felt his hot breath fan over her sensitive skin. He looked up at her; a man depraved. She nodded at him watching as he licked his lips. Roman's lips caressed her skin. His warm tongue licked her, ending at her clit. Nodin gasped, her fingers flexing into his shoulder. Roman paused looking at her over her pulsing cunt. "Keep going," Nodin encouraged. Roman licked her once more, then again and again. Nodin's head tilted back as her world shrank down to the feeling of Roman's tongue on her pussy.

Roman's strong warm tongue dipped into her core, licking at her nectar. Her fingers dug into his skin. Roman licked and sucked at her, taking breaks to lick at her clit, and once again he fucked her with his tongue.

Roman stuck his tongue deep into her cunt, sucking at her throbbing clit. Nodin screamed through her teeth, as her core clenched around his tongue, and she rubbed her cunt on his face as she rode out her orgasm, soaking his face. As her body collapsed against the bed, Roman looked at her, his face alight with satisfaction, his face dripping her orgasm. Roman held her eye contact as he licked her from his lips.

"Have you ever… with…" Roman trailed off looking at her. "Not… with …anyone," Nodin stumbled. "Do you ever.." He brushed a finger through her pulsing pussy. "Touch myself?" he asked. Roman nodded. "Yes," she hummed.

"Naughty girl. Roman held his finger tip at the entrance to her pussy, teasing her. "Do you?" Nodin nipped at her lips. "I have had sex before. Yes, I fuck my hand thinking of you." Roman slowly slipped his finger into her. His finger sat snugly in her cunt, filling up the space but not stretching her out. "Can you take another?" Nodin breathed. Roman kneeled between her thighs, his cock tenting up his pants. Roman answered by slipping in another finger. "You are so fucking wet," Roman growled as he gently wiggled his fingers in her. Slowly he pumped his fingers building her up, but not getting her all the way there.

"Roman." Nodin wiggled under his touch, craving more. "Another?" Roman smiled delighting in her struggle. "Yes," Nodin moaned. He slipped a third finger in between one thrust and the next. His thumb found her clit rubbing it as he pumped his fingers faster in her pussy. "You make such pretty sounds. Do you hear yourself?" Nodin held her breath to listen to the wet sound her cunt was making as his fingers thrust into her over and over.

"Yes." Roman rubbed slow circles around her clit, curling his fingers up and pressing into the soft muscles of her cunt. Nodin moaned deeply as he worked a second orgasm out of her. Nodin was left buzzing and panting as her body shook with the after-effect of her orgasm. Roman smirked at her as he stuck his fingers in his mouth, cleaning off his fingers.

Roman slid to the end of the bed, shoving his hand down his pants. Nodin tried to protest as he stroked himself. He dropped his pants to the floor, and Nodin's eyes widened at the sight of his cock springing free. He cock bounced a little, large and pink. The veins bulged at her, begging to be released. Roman crawled towards her. "How does she feel?" He cupped a hand over her throbbing cunt. "Good." Nodin could not take her eyes off his cock. "Ready?" He thrust into his hand, jerking himself off. "Yes." Roman spat on his hand, rubbing his saliva all over the head of his cock.

Slowly, he teased the head of his cock over her cunt, pushing gently through the folds of her pussy. Roman paused as it kissed up against her cunt. Roman pushed gently into her, Nodin gasped at the pressure. He was stretching her out already, feeling huge in her. Roman stopped letting her adjust to his size. She felt the gentle pulsing of his cock, it felt burning hot. "You take me so well," Roman cooed, kissing her face. "More," Nodin breathed. Roman sank a little deeper into her cunt. "Fuck you feel like heaven," Roman moaned.

Roman worked his way to the hilt, his body leaning into her. "Good?" Roman asked, watching her. "Very," Nodin moaned, biting into her lip. Roman thrust into her, slowly at first letting her enjoy his size. He picked up speed, thrusting into her. Nodin's mind went numb with blinding pleasure, her core tightening around his cock. "Nodin," Roman moaned through gritted teeth. "Roman. I'm gonna…" Her sentence was cut off by a body-rocking orgasm, and Nodin bit down on Roman's shoulder.

Roman rutted into her, following her over the edge with his own orgasm filling her cunt with his hot cum. Roman slumped into her, resting his head on her shoulder. His cock still sat deep inside her cunt. "Mea fera dea," he said into her skin.

After their breathing had calmed, their bodies coming down from the high, Roman pulled out of her, letting his seed spill out onto his bed. Roman got out of bed, grabbing his shirt from the day before, using it to clean up his cum from her cunt. He leaned over and kissed her, smiling.

Once they were all cleaned up, they curled up together enjoying the warmth of his body. Nodin fell back asleep in his arms.

25

Nodin woke up with the sun shining across the floor. Nodin rolled over, stretching out her arm behind her. The bed was cold and empty. In an instant, her heart stopped and then shattered. Nodin fell back against the bed, he had left her here alone, and now he would ignore her after she had given him her trust with a piece of her soul. She had bared her heart to him and he was going to drop her like a hot coal now he had gotten what he wanted.

Her fingers brushed the edge of paper, slicing the side of her finger. Hissing at the paper cut she sat up. A book sat on Roman's pillow, a piece of paper sticking out of it. Tugging the letter from the pages Nodin flipped it open with a heavy heart.

Morning beautiful.
I had an early class. I hope you slept well.
Thank you for last night.
I think you would enjoy this book.
Rex tenebrarum

Nodin folded the paper back up, slipping it in the front of the book. She hugged it to her chest, her heart fluttering under its pages. Nodin got dressed leaving a note of her own on his desk.

~

Nodin clutched the book Roman had given her that morning, to her chest all day. Wishing to sink into it, but working through her classes with her friends. Nodin had caught up on the class she had missed due to her lack of sleep. Performing much better in her classes she was no longer under the eagle eye of her professors. Making sure to toe the line of performing well enough to be forgotten.

She filled her day with her friends' laughter; filling the hours with school; and friends and learning. Hoping that just maybe for a moment she could want to be here and not at the lake. For just one moment to live here, and not in the corners of her mind. Rather than have dinner with her friends, Nodin packed up her dinner, a sandwich, an apple, a cookie, and a cup of spice soda.

She packed her meal into her bag and made her way to the lake, this time choosing to walk to the forest's edge on foot. Reaching the edge of the forest, between one branch and another, she jumped to the lake.

Settling down by her tree, Nodin finally opened the book. It was a biographical journal of an old elven poet, from before they had retreated from the world. Marked in the margins was a distinctive print -Roman's.

He had annotated the book with his inner thoughts. With several different colors of ink, Nodin could even see how his writing had improved over time. He had loved this book for many years. Staring at his writing, seeing the visual impression of his voice.

She hadn't even finished the first passage when the scent of earthy water lilies danced on the wind. She looked up to see Roman emerging from the underbrush. Folding his long limbs under him, Roman settled beside her. "What do you think?" Roman asked, tilting his head at the book in her hand.

"It's amazing." Nodin smiled at him, stunning him with her exuberance. Nodin faltered, feeling suddenly awkward under Roman's gaze. "Nodin," Roman whispered. "Yes?" She looked up at him. "About last night." Nodin's heart guttered in her chest. "Last night," Nodin repeated.

"Are we good?" Roman looked nervous to her, it was barely perceivable but to her it was clear. "Yes." What did *are we good* mean? Nodin's face settled into a pleasant mask, smiling at him. "Good cause for me, it wasn't just…a meaningless fuck." Roman ran his hand through his hair, stumbling over his words. A spark lit in Nodin's chest, melting her mask to the young woman underneath. "Do you meaninglessly fuck many people?" Nodin smirked at the shock on his face.

"No…no… I… don't but I know some people do and it wasn't like that to me…because I feel too much for you." Nodin was shocked at his confession. "Feel what too much?" Nodin asked dumbly. Her heart hammered in her chest, and Roman's mouth twitched with fear gleaming in his eyes. Nodin let the silence stretch on waiting for Roman to answer. "That I love you."

Roman's words bounced around her head. "Love?" The word was barely out of her mouth when the quiet sound of voices filtered through the trees. Roman and Nodin turned around, searching for the source. "What was that?" Roman whispered to her. A few more voices found their ears, getting louder. The snapping of twigs under feet echoed through the branches. Nodin's blood screamed in her ears as she scooped up her stuff and darted across the rocky beach to the trees on the other side.

Roman was right on her heels as Nodin flew into the under-brush. Roman stopped behind her, turning around. Hiding under the dark leaves of a bush, Roman looked back at the beach. Coming out from the trees was a figure that turned Nodin's blood to ice. Ivor. *Slimy bastard.*

Nodin watched as Ivor stomped around the beach, kicking rocks into the lake. It was the other heirs and their cohort of brainless admirers. Ivor jumped, swinging his arms up, latching onto the branch of a tree, and pulled his chin to the bark. The group whistled and chanted at him as he executed four more pull-ups. Letting go he smiled at the group in a grim slash of his lips. Nodin watched Roman out of the corner of her eye, he was watching the group intently.

The group started to settle down, Nodin felt the lake protesting at the intruders. Ivor and his group started to rip apart the weave as they practiced their parlor tricks the mortals passed as magic. "Let's go, they will stay there for a while." Roman turned to her, taking her hand. Nodin turned her back on the lake, mourning the untouched weave that was lost.

"Nodin." Roman tugged at her hand. With a single glance back at the heirs, who were pushing each other and laughing, she followed Roman. Roman broke into a run, letting her hand go to navigate the thick underbrush. Nodin ran behind him letting her hand trail behind her, slipping along the weave, hiding their tracks.

The forest got thicker as they ran deeper into the dark. Nodin found the branches soothing, but Roman seemed to struggle with the thicket. Branches batted at him, and he swatted back letting them snap back behind him. Nodin dodged and weaved around the thicket with ease.

Nodin felt the ripples in the weave before she saw the tree; it was a gnarly old thing, gripping to the earth out of spite. The weave around the tree was shredded, drifting around in ribbons. Roman ran straight for the tangle of branches none the wiser. The tears in the weave were old, a story to be told, over hundreds of years old. The damage was irreparable even by the most gifted elven weavers.

Nodin lunged forward, reaching for Roman to stop him but she was too late as they barreled under the tree. Nodin felt the grating feeling of the broken weave, but with some luck they did not encounter any void holes.

Nodin let out a breath as Roman pushed through the last of

the branches; stepping past the snapping branches. A branch swung and bit into her back, and Nodin lurched into Roman at the impact.

Roman stumbled past several more trees before stopping to check on Nodin. "Are you okay?" he panted, stopping. "Yes, let's keep going." They walked slowly through the trees. Nodin felt the cool air licking at her skin, her clothing ripped wide open. "Did the branch get you?" Roman stopped, and leaned against the tree, panting his lungs burning in his chest.

"Only a little." Nodin's throat burned with the bite of the cold air. "Let me see." He launched his body off the tree walking towards her. "No, I am ok." Nodin stepped back from him. The panic that gripped Nodin's heart was stronger than the guilt coursing through her veins.

"I just want to make sure you aren't hurt." Roman kept moving towards her. Nodin's heart stuttered in her chest, her lungs refusing to take in air. "I'm not." Nodin's voice sounded hollow to her ears. "Please. I'm worried about you." Roman's hands pulled gently at her sleeve. Nodin had not fooled herself that she would make it all the way through her time at school without suspicion.

She knew she had to be careful not to be found. She had failed, she had let her vigilance slip, Roman's heart softening her walls. Nodin debated jumping to the safety of her room right before his eyes. The guilt had rooted her to the ground, her feelings for the man that would ruin her life kept her standing before him.

Roman side stepped, slipping behind her, the seconds before her world blew up slipping through her fingers. Nodin felt Roman's fingers pulling aside her leaf-tangled hair. Roman started to lift the back of her clothes. As the air danced on her back Nodin panicked, her legs waking up.

Nodin bolted forward a few steps turning to face him. She searched her mind for an excuse. "I said …" Nodin started, fumbling for words. "Your back." Roman had gone white, frozen in shock. His hands still lifted in the air from wear he hand lifted her shirt.

Something in her broke, deep in her soul. Nodin blinked, letting the tears fall down her face, Roman just looked at her like she had eaten dead rotten roadkill from a highway in front of him.

Nodin blinked, wrapping the weave around her, and when she opened her eyes she was back in her room. She stood there numb, till her limbs buckled out from under her.

26

Nodin stayed on the floor in a crumpled pile, her heart numb in her chest. Slowly, she dragged herself off the floor, stiffly pulling off her clothing. She turned her back to her mirror, twisting to look at her skin. Across the middle of her back was an angry scratch from the branch. The skin around it puffed up in a nasty red welt. Her gaze dipped down her spine, stopping only a couple of inches lower. Buried deep in her skin were ghostly leaves. Ivy leaves.

Starting at the base of her spine, under her skin grew a vine, twisting and sprouting ivy leaves. She brushed a finger over the skin, feeling the slight ridge of the plant, as it grew up her spine the vine sank deeper into her skin, getting muddy and blurry from the milky skin. The top leaves were no more than green blobs deep in her skin. The only mark of her elven blood.

The vines on their backs reflected the life they had lived, the oldest elves covered from head to toe with their vines. Nodin's fingers brushed over the two brown, dead leaves that sat in the scoop of her back. The loss of her parents. That grief had marked her skin, changing her permanently.

Her leaves would never be as big or vibrant as her full-blooded family, in their eyes sullied by her mother's mortal blood. She had given up the secret of her people. An outcast for her blood as it was she would be ostracized for revealing the closely guarded secret of her birth. That in fact halflings existed.

It had been many dark years of war that had plagued the world before the elves had retreated to the wilds. Mortals craved the power of elven blood, going to every length to steal the power for themselves. Mortals had captured and tortured the elves, draining their blood and experimenting on them till death freed them from the pain. When they were not fruitful, they resorted to raping every elf they could get their hands on.

The monstrosities they enacted on the female elves were wiped from the books, but not the memories. With years passing and not a single child born from the two bloodlines, the mortals forfeit that it was not possible to sire a halfling. It was soon after that a treaty was drafted and the elves isolated themselves to the wilds. The scars they endured never faded, the rift between them vast.

The mortals in their greed had overseen one small detail, that the elven woman could use the weave to render themselves infertile. The elven woman had ripped their wombs from their bodies to ensure they never sired a halfling, to keep the weave from the mortals grasp.

With the absence of the elves, mortals found a way to wield the weave for themselves. Ripping it apart to form their abominations, to fill their greed. No longer under the watchful eyes of the elves, they tore the world apart, damaging the very thing the elves swore to protect. Nodin had failed to protect her people, she had let slip that a halfling lived among them.

Pain bloomed in her chest, and Nodin let out a strangled cry. Her fist embedded into the mirror, the glass slicing open her hand. Her rage-filled tears streamed down her face, all twisted and red with fury. Nodin toppled her desk, smashing her chair. She snatched at the clothes in her wardrobe, ripping them from the hangers, littering them all over her floor. Nodin's pain took form in her body and ransacked her room. The only thing untouched was her books.

Nodin looked at the books, the worn pages of the book Roman had given her, calling her name. In a last gasp of pain, she swept her hand over the shelf, sending all her books to the floor. Nodin fell to the floor with them, whimpering as she held the soft bound book to her chest. The last and only piece of Roman she had left.

Nodin curled up on the floor in a pile of blankets and shredded clothes, her tears silently falling as her exhausted body caught up with her. Nodin lay there, letting the throbbing pain in her hand keep her awake. She laid there numb, and felt the pain in her hand, punishment for what she had done. For what she had lost.

~

Nodin was unsure how long she had stayed in her nest, the broken remnants of her life around her. She had certainly missed many classes, that she was sure of, and her roommates had come to her door seeking her. She had convinced the wood of the door to root and grow, entangling with the wood of the door frame locking everyone out. Roman's book lived in her grasp, locked in her fingers, the only thing keeping her heart beating.

Nodin slipped into sleep, and her nightmares returned with vengeance, except this time she didn't fight them. She embraced them. She deserved to be haunted by her past.

27

Nodin awoke from a nightmare, soaked in cold sweat. The sound of voices floated under the door. They were not the gentle voices of her worried roommates. Nodin ground her teeth, andand gripped the book to her chest, unable to let it go, but unable to open its pages.

It wasn't long till a knock echoed around her room. Nodin blocked it out. The roots on her door grew stronger at the intrusion. "Come on, princess. Don't deprive the world of your smile for too long." Lock's voice floated through the door. A couple of the roots broke off, falling to the floor. Nodin blinked at the door. Did she remember who she was? It felt like a lifetime had passed, that the woman she was before had died and this body had been born from the ash.

Nodin heard the sound of Lock's head hitting the door with a dull thud. A smile tugged at her lips, twisting the muscles in her face. "Just come out and talk for a minute," Sullan's voice joined Lock's. "We aren't leaving till we see your beautiful face," Kyrin called from farther away. "Yeah, we might not leave anyways, these couches are way better." Lock's voice retreated into the common room, the light edge she missed coming back to his voice.

Slowly, Nodin lifted herself from the floor. She swept her hand over the roots, they crumbled to ash under her touch. Leaning against the door frame she let the door open just enough to peek through it. Sitting by the fire were her roommates, and with them were the backs of four heads. Lock, Kyrin, Sullen, and Roman. No one was looking her way, all whispering to each other.

Lock leaned over to Ascelin, whispering something to her, and she leaned back, a light giggle dancing through the air. She had a glowing blush peppered across her cheeks. Lock was flirting with her, Nodin smiled at his shameless attempt. Nodin slipped out of her room, and stood there silently watching them.

"Nodin." At Roman's breathy voice, the room fell silent as everyone turned around to face her. Once again she was frozen in place, staring at Roman who walked towards her slowly, as if she was a spooked wild animal. Maybe she was. He looked horrible, his skin was pale, clothes rumbled, and his eyes swam with a hundred emotions. "Can we please talk?" Roman watched her, his eyes searching hers.

Nodin pushed her door open with her foot, disappearing into the darkness. Roman followed her in, fumbling for a candle in the dark. Nodin reached for the weave and the candle that had remained on her table sparked to life. The small yellow flame scattered shadows across the room. Roman looked around her trashed room, taking in the bare pain it expressed.

"What is it?" Nodin asked, not looking at him. "Why didn't you tell me?" Roman looked at her, and she felt his gaze dancing over her skin. "Tell you what?" Nodin's heart was breaking every second she stood before him. "About…" Roman waved his hand up and down indicating her. Nodin didn't say a word as she looked over at him, wrapping her arms around her, gripping her elbows. "You don't trust me?" Roman asked, looking at the floor.

"I don't owe you anything." Nodin let her voice harden, turning into the pain and the anger, letting the anguish be drowned out. "Tell me!" Roman raised his voice, soaked in desperation. Under her mask, her heart beat stuttered in her chest. "Please," Roman whispered, begging.

"It's not my secret to tell," Nodin finally answered, deflated. The damn let loose in her chest and her words came tumbling out faster than her tongue could keep up. "If I tell anyone… the amount of people who would suffer because of it." Nodin's voice strangled in her chest.

"I won't tell anyone. I promise." Roman took a tentative step forward, one hand over his chest, and one reaching towards her. "You don't know that!" Nodin gasped. "You don't know…" Nodin continued.

"I love you. You! Not what you do. Not where you are. Not what you are. You." Roman cut her off. Roman paused, panting slightly, he gulped down deep breaths of air. Without a word Nodin turned slowly, her back facing him. Nodin gripped her shirt tightly, letting her shaking hands lift the fabric. Slowly, inch by inch, it revealed her back. Roman didn't make a sound, he took in her back for several heart beats.

Nodin jumped slightly as the tip of his finger brushed her back. Gently he skimmed his fingertips over the skin. His nimble fingers traced her vines. "You're an elf," Roman guessed in barely a whisper.

"No." Nodin glanced back over her shoulder, watching him admire her skin, "A halfling." Nodin held her breath, watching Roman carefully, and wrapped herself in the weave desperate for any comfort. "Impossible." Nodin felt the tip of his fingers dig a little deeper into her skin looking closer at the leaves under her skin. It took him some time to see that her vines were sunk a little deeper in her skin, and smaller than a full-blooded elf.

"If anyone…" Nodin started, pulling her shirt down. "If anyone found out it would start a war on elves, leading to their destruction." Nodin turned to face him, looking up at him. "Worse. The whole world would be ripped apart." Roman looked at her his mossy brown eyes shining. "You are safe with me." Roman tucked her shirt down, smoothing it out.

Roman spent the evening with her cleaning up her room, returning it to its original state.

28

Everyday the part of Nodin that expected Roman to spill her secret shrank. He never did. *He will, eventually.* The deepest parts of her mind haunted her. Roman didn't press her for more information about her heritage, nor bring up the subject in general. The one thing he did change was his reading material. She had noticed that he was reading more books authored by elves, even recommending many to her.

Ivor had yet to visit the lake again, but his single visit had fractured the safety. Every time Nodin was there, she kept looking over her shoulder waiting for him to come storming out of the underbrush. It took Nodin over a week to heal the damage to the weave his friends had caused.

Nodin every now and then felt the scar in the weave, she was sure one of her kin could have done a much better job, but she was not her kin. She was only a halfling, and one who had been cut off from her elven blood from a young age. Her fondest memories were the hours spent with her father learning about her history, how to use the weave, but she had much left to learn when she lost them.

113

It was a short month that slipped through her fingers in the blink of an eye. The last week before the school's winter break was brutal, the professors putting them through their paces. Even leading to one-fourth of Nodin's class being asked to leave the school for under performance. No year had been left unscathed, with students from every year being told to leave permanently.

Nodin hoped some of the heirs would get cut, especially Ivor, excluding Roman who she often forgot was an heir. The last night before everyone at the school left to see their families, Nodin and her roommates spent an evening on the floor before the fire relaxing together, enjoying one of their many homemade face masks.

Nodin was staying at the school, the only one of the four women to stay. Over eighty percent of the school and faculty were leaving for the two week break. Despite the lack of occupants, the school was decorated all month long for Yule.

Nodin waited with bated breath that morning, watching from an alcove in the main hall as streams of students left. Roman was staying behind with her, the first year he didn't return to his family. Nodin had heard about his mothers complaints at the change of plans.

Roman's dorm mates were all leaving too, leaving both dorms empty, Nodin had packed up a bag to spend the two weeks in Roman's dorm. Not that it was much different as she spent most nights sleeping in his bed, occasionally they spent the night in hers, and rarely they spent it apart.

Once the halls had emptied Nodin made her way to Roman's dorm, knocking on the door, the halls silent. "Come in," Roman called through the door. Swinging the door open she walked into the warm room, a fire blazing in the hearth, a picnic of food spread out on the living room table.

"So normally before we leave for Yule we deep clean the dorm, I however said I would do it since I was staying. I was thinking we could do it together and make it fun. I hope that's ok?" Roman launched into his spiel as she entered the room. Nodin looked towards his dorm mates rooms. "Oh, not their rooms, they are already done," Roman clarified. "Sounds good." Nodin dropped her bag to the food, embracing Roman.

Nodin helped Roman completely deep clean the dorm, the time filled with laughter and snacks. Late in the evening, Roman had disappeared to the dining hall to procure them dinner.

Roman set a delicious-smelling container in front of her, ripping open the lid to find a pilling heap of coconut rice and spicy fried tofu tempting her. Digging in with vigor she spooned the hot food into her mouth. After dinner, Nodin was curled up on the couch as Roman finished up the rest of the cleaning.

Nodin got up and walked over to the frosted window, poking at the crispy plant that sat in a large pot on the windowsill. "Oh, that can get thrown out," Roman said, reaching for the pot.

Nodin batted his hand away. Nodin ran her hand over the

leaves of the plant. Deep in its roots the plant held on to life, and Nodin coaxed the weave through the roots of the plant, slowly it's leaves turned to a dark green, lifting, coming back to life.

"Amazing," Roman whispered, looking at her in awe. Blushing, Nodin fidgeted under his gaze. It had been a long time since she had so blatantly used her magic in front of another. Spending the rest of the night watching the snow drift past the window, wrapped up in each other's arms. Late in the night, the fire was no more than embers, they moved from the couch and to Roman's room.

29

"Do you want to see something magical?" Nodin asked, over breakfast, they sat in the empty dining hall. The large buffet table that normally graced the room, had been replaced by a much smaller one. "Absolutely," Roman talked through a mouth full of food. Nodin wrinkled her nose at the chewed food in his mouth.

Laughing at her he opened his mouth fully to gross her out even more, Nodin couldn't help but laugh at him. Roman swallowed his mouthful before continuing, "what do you have in mind?"

"We are going to the lake," Nodin smiled at him, giving away that she had a plan. "The lake is amazing and magical, but I go there regularly," Roman pointed out. "Trust me," Nodin challenged. Roman nodded, turning back to his food. After breakfast Roman started on his way to make his way to the lake, as he normally would.

"Roman," Nodin called not following him. She held out her hand. He stopped and took it, starting to pull her with him. "Deep breath." Nodin started to wrap the weave around them, taking her time to ensure that Roman made a safe trip with her.

Roman stumbled back from her, taking in the lake around them. "You can just…" Roman stuttered, reaching down to pick up one of the stones. Roman ran his fingers over the smooth stone, grounding himself that he in fact had moved from one place to the next. "That was magical." Roman looked up at her.

"It hasn't even started yet," Nodin smiled at him. She reached over and dusted the few snowflakes that had landed in his hair. Gently, the snow started to fall around them, melting into the ground.

Nodin took his hand, guiding him over to the edge of the water, walking confidently over the surface. Roman faulted at the edge of the water. He looked up at her standing on the edge of the water taking a deep breath, he took a step out onto the water. Nodin smiled, tugging on his hand, she ran letting her legs fly over the water. Roman ran along with her, calling his enjoyment to the sky.

Standing, panting, in the middle of the lake she smiled at him. Roman's cheeks were flushed from running through the frozen air. Deep in her soul, she tugged at the weave, creating a theatrical show for Roman.

The water around them started to bubble, rolling and boiling under their feet. Slowly a thin wall of water rose around them in a circle. As the water closed over their heads, the water under them began to sink. As they disappeared under the surface in their clear bubble, Roman's hands gripped hers tightly.

As their little bubble swam through the water, Roman watched in awe at the underwater world. It got very dark as they neared the bottom of the lake, and Nodin guided the bubble along the lake floor, moving around the large rocks and plants. Roman gasped as a large school of fish swam past, glowing purple, the water around them filled with pale blue light glowing in wisps. Even in the dim water, Roman could see the dark void that opened up in the lake floor. "Are we going down there?" Roman's hand pointed to the chasm below. "Absolutely."

Roman gripped Nodin's hand as they sank into the chasm, their bubble bathed in complete darkness. Nodin listened to the low keening of the deep water, far from silent. The gentle clicking sounds of the aquatic life talking to each other. Several long minutes passed as they kept sinking. Nodin smiled at Roman as they leveled out as they moved along the bottom of the chasm.

Roman peaked out through the bubble searching the dark for some movement in the deep water. Slowly they began to rise to the rocky wall of the chasm. Through the darkness Roman could see an eerie glow shine through the dark. The blue-green light danced deep in the chasm, they were headed right to it.

Then the bubble broke the surface, popping around them as their feet hit the rocky bottom of the cave. Roman looked around taking in the cave around him, the walls lined with glowing algae casting its blue-green light all around them. The walls were peppered with small flowers, adding their golden glow to the light. The cave was right out of a fairy tale, filled with small creatures walking around the air-pocket cave, even birds flying around in the air.

It was a whole ecosystem, untouched, living deep below the earth. "Follow me," Nodin forged ahead, picking a path through the large plants and boulders, coming to a secondary pool deep into the cave. Roman stopped as a bird fluttered in his face, it looked like a blue robin instead of feathers covering its body it had fur, its large blue wings fluttering behind its body. The wings kept its small body in the air the brilliant blue of a butterfly's, even mirroring the shape of a butterfly's.

Roman held out his hand to the small bird, it regarded him for a moment before flying off. "This has been here the whole time?" Nodin stopped at the edge of the pool, and Roman saw that it was much deeper than he had first thought. "I would guess this cave has been here longer than mortals have walked the earth," Nodin commented. Something moved in the deep water of the pool. Roman stepped back as a massive form rose to the surface. Nodin didn't blink as a head lifted from the water. It was a creature, its bright orange eyes blinking at the two people in its home. Its scaled head was huge, the dark green skin covered in the glowing algae of the walls.

"What is it?" Roman hissed through his teeth, not taking his eyes off the massive creature. "He," Nodin corrected, and reached out a hand towards the nose of the creature. He closed his eyes as Nodin's hand touched his skin, letting out a breath through his nostrils, blowing mist at them. "What is he?" Roman didn't dare move. "A sea dragon." Nodin rubbed the scaled nose of the beast. "A dragon?" Roman asked, eyeing the large beast.

"He won't hurt you." Nodin grabbed Roman's hand, placing it on the dragons cool skin -next to hers. Roman's heart hammered in his ears, he was touching a creature that hadn't been written about in centuries, let alone seen. The sea dragon opened his eyes, letting out a low sound, that rumbled through Roman's bones.

Nodin smiled as the sea dragon sank back under the surface of his home. "Do not harm this place and you are welcome to visit," a deep voice echoed around the walls. Roman flinched at the voice, and looked over the pool. The sea dragon was pulling its large body out of the water on the other side of the pool. Roman nodded at him before he disappeared deep into the cave.

"He can talk," Roman choked looking at Nodin as she laughed at him. "Many creatures can talk, not just humanoids." Nodin and Roman spent hours walking through the wonders of the cave. Each crevice and corner of the cave holds some new wonder.

Nodin wrapped her arms around Roman's neck, pulling him close, and kissing him under the glowing ceiling. Gently she wrapped the weave around them, bringing them to the beach, the snow having built up by several inches. "Thank you," Roman whispered against her lips. "It's important that you…umm…don't tell anyone." Nodin stepped back, the snow crunching under her foot. "I know. If anyone found out about it, it would be destroyed." Roman stepped back too. "Gotta listen to the wise sea dragon." Roman kissed her forehead.

~

Roman and Nodin spent a couple of days in bed where Nodin found out that Roman had a passion for art. He had several notebooks filled with pencil sketches and watercolor skies. Nodin smiled at several portraits of herself in the pages. He had spent hours yesterday with Nodin in his arms, sketching the cave in extensive detail. "Want to see more?" Nodin shifted in the sheets looking at him.

"I'd love to go to the cave again." Roman sat up looking at her, the notebook falling to the floor. "A different one," Nodin slipped from the bed, grabbing her clothes. "There is another cave?" Roman stepped into his pants. "Many."

Nodin bundled herself up in many layers, reaching her hand out to Roman. He slipped his hand in hers and smiled at her, she wrapped the weave around them and within the blink of an eye, they were deep in the woods. Only a light smattering of snow had made it to the forest floor, while the rest of the world had been buried under a blanket of snow.

"We aren't gonna just appear in the cave?" Roman asked, looking around at the trees. "The journey is half the fun." Nodin walked ahead, skipping through the trees. Roman followed her. "You know there is just as much beauty here as in the sea dragons cave," Nodin said, stopping by a large moss-covered tree. "You just have to look." She looked up at the tree, her fingers tracing the branches through the air.

Roman studied the trees trying to see what she saw. He watched as the snow drifted through the branches landing on the moss, sparkling in the dappled light shining through the forest; and then he saw it. All the life breathing around him. "I see it," he whispered, watching the world around him.

"Come on." Nodin pulled him deeper and deeper into the forest until she came to a huge gnarled tree that stood over large rocks. Nodin smiled slyly at Roman before ducking under the roots and disappearing. Roman followed her blindly into the depths of the earth.

Roman shuffled along the damp tunnel, following Nodin's back disappearing down the tunnel. Nodin stopped in the dark, waiting for him. Nodin looked over her shoulder at him, and Roman rested his hand on the small of her spine. "Ready?" Roman nodded, kissing her cheek. "Close your eyes," Nodin whispered. Nodin guided Roman through the mouth of the cave.

"Open," Nodin whispered in Romans ear, and he opened his eyes. Roman was blinded by the glimmering light emanated from the cave. The walls were lined with fist-sized glimmering gems shining in blue and green light. Huge chunks of obsolescent white crystals rose from the floor and ceiling, towering over his head.

Nodin watched as Roman took it all in, frozen in place. The

long winding cave dove into the earth at a steep slope. A deep blue and purple glow emanating from the end of the cave. A pale blue glow bounced around in the closest white pillar, it danced at the surface.

The light checked out Nodin and Roman before slipping out of the crystal, a small blue butterfly made of light flew up to them. It fluttered in front of Roman's face, slowly getting closer to him, before darting away and fluttering around Nodin. The butterfly left them flying deep into the cave, each pillar it passed lit up with the pale blue light. Slowly the butterfly's sleeping in the crystal woke up, following the first.

The whole cave was lit with a cloud of butterflies, a swirling storm of little wings. The cave was full of butterflies, settling on the gem-crusted walls around them. Several settled on Nodin, lighting up her raven hair. Nodin turned to Roman smiling, he was bathed in blue light, one curious butterfly sitting on the back of his hand.

Nodin and Roman slowly made their way deeper into the cave, the hues of the walls getting darker. Fewer white pillars, slowly being replaced by murky green ones, rising so high they disappeared into the ceiling. Nodin darted around the pillars, climbing over the large crystal obstacles. Roman bent down picking up a rough chunk of red stone, flipping it over in his palm.

It filled his palm and he held it up looking into the surface. "This is a ruby!" he yelled running over to show Nodin. "It is." She picked up the piece. "Do you know how much this is worth?" Roman looked around the cave spotting more and more value in the stones lying littered around them.

"Do you know how much the value will fall the second you remove it from the cave?" Nodin looked at him with a sharp look. Did he want to destroy such a beautiful place? She thought he got it after the sea dragon cave, but clearly, he couldn't sell anything from that cave. This one all he could see was the money. This cave didn't have an ancient beast watching over it.

Roman looked at her, seeing the judgment written all over her face. "This is one of the last caves like this, the rest have been stripped by the greed of mortals," Nodin snapped, turning from him. Roman's heart stuttered in his chest. Nodin refused to look at him, fighting back tears for all the world had lost.

"I didn't think," Roman whispered, he set the stone back down on the ground. "Nodin." He rubbed his hands over her shoulders. "Please look at me." Nodin turned to him gazing, at his sad eyes. "Yes?"

"I understand." He looked around the cave. "If you take anything from here, what's stopping one from taking everything? Then this cave no longer exists, and the world loses something more important than what the mortal's would gain." Roman kissed her forehead. "They already took so much." Nodin leaned into him. "Plus where would the butterflies go?" Roman added with a smile.

"Do you know why I go to school?" Nodin asked, wrapping

herself in his arms. "No, I don't." Nodin took a moment to gather her thoughts. "Because if the mortals saw me use the weave without having been to school, I would be tossed in a cell and forgotten about." Nodin bite through her words, letting the anger sink in. "But elves are exempt," Roman countered. "They have shunned me, and if I told the mortals I'm an elf…" Nodin didn't need to explain anymore, Roman understood.

Together, they stood in the dark cave, enjoying the silence. Taking in the wonder of the world around them. Nodin opened her eyes, the blue light glowing around them, the butterflies had landed on them; coating them in a blanket of light. Nodin watched the gentle butterflies flex their wings on Roman's back. Breaking apart, the butterflies dispersed around them in a mist of wings, Roman smiled at her.

Deep from the crowd of wings, two dark blue moths flew from the depths of the cave. Circling the two mortals, the moths watched them, Nodin held out her hand for the large animals. One settled down on her hand taking up her whole hand covering her wrist, Nodin looked at the moth. It flicked its fuzzy antenna at her, something deep in her soul stirred connecting with it on a deeper level. Roman copied her, holding out his hand, the second moth settling in his palm.

The moths stayed in their hands for several minutes, they watched the animals rest, before fluttering their dark wings and leaving. Left behind in their hands was a gem, the size of a tear drop, both gems sparkled with a light blue light glowing from within. Roman tilted his hand to let the gem fall to the floor, trying to return it to the cave. "Wait." Nodin lunged forward cupping his hand in hers. "It's a gift from the cave," Nodin said, tucking the gem in her pocket. "I get to keep it?" Roman's face lit up looking at the small rock.

"You do." Nodin nodded. Roman placed it carefully in his breast pocket, tapping it to ensure it was safe. "I feel so special." Nodin and Roman walked back through the cave, hand in hand till they reached the outside world. Night had fallen in the time they had been in the cave, the snow thicker on the ground, the top iced over. Opting to walk through the snow towards the snow, enjoying the cool air.

30

Nodin loved spending the days and nights with Roman, getting lost in the pages of books, or in each other's thoughts. After Nodin and Roman had eaten through every word in the books they had, Roman took Nodin to the school library. Spending a day in between the shelves of books. Between the two of them, they filled a whole table with books to read.

Nodin found a small book, the history of the families, Nodin didn't have to wonder what families it was referring to. Each chapter was titled with a family name, all of which she recognized. Under each name, the family's motto was inscribed. Mandora; ad perpetuam memoriam. To the perpetual memory. Daunte; ad augusta per angusta. Through difficulties to honors. Bakhart; humilitas occidit superbiam. Humility conquers pride. Potman; res non verba. Deeds not words. Hoewlman; ubi dubium ibi libertas. Where there is doubt there is freedom. Van'Hight; absens haeres non erit. An absent person will not be heir. Nodin returned the book to the shelf.

Roman lit the candles around their table, the warm light

dancing over the walls. "I have a surprise for you." Roman peeked at her over the stack of books. "Really?" Nodin smiled at him. "Yes, my sweet lullaby. You have been showing me all these beautiful places. I have one to show you." Roman stood up offering her his hand.

Nodin smiled, slipping her hand in his, and placed the book in her hand down on the table. Nodin gripped the metal base of the candle, lighting up the maze of bookshelves that Roman led her through. At the very back of the library stood a pair of large wooden doors.

The weave guttered around Roman's fingers before he tapped the doors. He had refrained from using his magic around her, Nodin realized this was the first time he had used it in her presence for all of Yule. He had not used his magic since classes had stopped. Nodin's heart warmed as the doors swung open with a deep howl of the hinges.

Nodin wrinkled her nose as the air was filled with dust, the air smelled old. The smell of old paper, and dust bunnies. Nodin walked through the doors, a thick layer of dust on the floor. The room had been undisturbed for decades, except for the small trail of footprints from the main door and around the shelves. Roman marched into the room, leaving behind a trail of footprints matching the ones already on the floor. They were his footprints.

"What is this place?" Nodin asked, looking at the vaulted ceilings. The bookshelves were packed with books, each shelf rising to the muraled ceiling. Painted on the ceiling in muted tones was a woman standing in a lake. Her long white dress blended with her white blonde hair, turning clear in the water, revealing her legs in the water, the lake's plants wrapped around her ankles.

"I'm not sure. I think it's a personal library. It's been locked for centuries." Roman ran his fingers over the spines of the old leather. Roman closed the doors behind them. Nodin looked back at the doors from this side; they were carved from clear crystal, though distorted, and the view into the school's library was clear.

Nodin turned to the shelves, climbing up the walnut ladder that was attached to the shelf, she scanned the titles. Almost everyone had an elven author. "Roman! Is this how you had so many books by elves?" Nodin twisted on the ladder, the movement causing it to slide along the railing. "Yes," Roman answered from among the shelves. Nodin pulled a heavy leather-bound text from the shelf, the leather worn but not cracked. As if the book had been paused in a time when it had been well loved.

"The school does have some texts by elves, but they are a select few and only fourth years get to read them." Roman appeared at the bottom of her ladder. Nodin stared at the title of the book, *The Dangerous of the Void,* maybe she could get some answers. Letting the book tumble through the air like a feather, settling gently on the floor.

Nodin searched the shelves for every and any book referencing the void, tears in the weave or the effects of mortal casting.

A slim black book tucked away on the top shelf snagged her attention. No author or title was embossed on the side, tilting the book out peaking at its cover Nodin's breath hitched. *Void Beasts.* The faded title stared back at her, still no author was evident on the cover.

Dropping the book to drift down to her pile her mind spun, it was spinning so fast she almost didn't spot the slim leather book hidden behind the other books. Curiosity gripped her heart, and she wrestled her fingers into the small space grasping at the pages. It took her several minutes to free the book from its dust cage.

The dark leather was creased with use, the leather strap wrapped around the book fraying. There was no title and no author anywhere on the book's cover. Leaning against the shelf she flipped open the book, the thick paper turning yellow, stained with water marks. In small neat print on the inside of the front cover was penned a name in dark ink. **Erebo Merle.**

Her father. She flipped through the pages, journal entry after journal entry, each dating two hundred years ago. She had known her father was older than her mother, elves lived much longer lives than mortals, four to five times longer. What was his journal doing here? He had never gone to school.

Nodin slid down the ladder, letting her feet skip over the rungs. She kept her nose deep in its pages, absentmindedly picking up her other books from the floor. "Roman!" She called deep into the room. He was nowhere to be found. Abandoning her books, tucking her fathers journal under her arm, she ran through the shelves.

The room was much larger than she had first thought, with alcoves and halls leading to secondary rooms leading off of the main room. This secret library was nearly double the size of the school's original library. *Or this is the original.* "Roman," Nodin called over the sound of her frantic footsteps. "Here," Roman's distant voice called from the far back of the room. As she reached the back of the library she turned down the last row of shelves. Romans head popped out of a shadowy nook she otherwise would have overlooked.

"There you are." Nodin panted, and slipped into the nook, between the shelves. The space opened up in front of her, she stepped in. Opening up before her was a massive office. A large desk stood in the middle, piled high with books and papers. Dried up ink pots, and broken feathers littered the top of the desk. Behind the desk stood a huge hexagon shelf spilling over with scrolls. Hanging on the back of the ornate wooden chair were several leather scroll cases, the leather and brass strap looped over the back of the chair.

The room was stuffy, the air thick with dust, and smelling of moth-eaten paper. Roman was looking through the books on the shelves. "Listen to this," Roman read from a paper he had scooped from the desk. "It is with a heavy heart that I lock away the archive. This vault of elven history must survive. The six families have declared the destruction of all elven literature. They want the history books wiped.

"The blood stain of their rule was removed. They have brain

washed an entire generation on the war they waged against us. We will not forget. We will not forgive. I hope that in time this archive will be found by open minds." Roman looked up at her. "It's dated fifty years before the elves left." Nodin looked at him, and tugged her fathers journal out from under her arm.

"We aren't the first ones here," Nodin waved the book in front of her face. "It's my fathers journal from two hundred years ago," Roman looked at the book. "Long after they looked this place away, listen to this." She opened the journal to the first page reading from the very first entry. "I don't know how this place has sat in the school for centuries undetected, but I could feel the archive that has been lost calling to me for years, and I have finally found it. I feel a great obligation to present it to the Elders, our history has been lost for too long, but I fear that its hiding place is for a reason. The school that is the heart of our downfall. I shall wait till I know why the archive choose now, choose to reveal itself to me."

Nodin flipped to half way through the book. "I am not the only one who has found the archive. I don't think it's another elf. If the archives are compromised I must save them." Nodin flipped to another page reading a short passage from the back of the book. "Romona agrees we should lock the archive and never return, I feel as though I should leave my mark among the history safeguarded here."

"Ramona is my mother, it's how they met." Nodin closed the book, hugging it to her chest. The words from the young version of her father treasured between the pages. "Why did it reveal itself to me?" Roman asked, looking around the office.

Nodin felt as though the walls were breathing around them, the weave caressing her cheek. "I am not an elf."

"Nor was my mother," Nodin pointed out. "But your father was and you are, do you think it's a coincidence that it showed itself to us?" Roman hinted at a deeper meaning with his tone. Nodin shut herself down from dissecting what he could possibly mean, what the archive could be telling them.

"I think the archive knows that you are an ally to the elves," Nodin offered up. "We have to be careful as well, to keep this place safe," Nodin added. "Even today it would be deemed too dangerous to leave standing, it would all get burned." Roman looked at her. They left the office, looking back at the library. The sheer size of the space hitting Nodin in the face, so many volumes of history, of her history saved and hidden.

It was even hidden from the elves, stored in the one place no one would suspect. In the oldest standing school of casting, right in the heart of the mortal world. *So little left.* All of the history, literary work, stories, and poems of the elves boiled down to one safe haven. The elves had epochs of history, all of it lost, only that which was stored in the memories of the elves left, and this one small pocket left.

Nodin would spend the rest of her long life, if she was blessed with her father's life span, and she would never read every single page stored here. In silent shock they walked back to the main doors, stopping to pick up their small pile of books. Roman paused before the doors. "Are you ok?" Nodin looked at him feeling numb. "This is all that is left," she whispered to him, she did not need to explain the sadness that gripped her voice. "I know." Roman closed his eyes.

The sun rose as Nodin and Roman walked from the library to Roman's dorm, their arms heavy with books and their hearts heavy with grief. They left all the books they had chosen from the school library on the table. Nodin was numb for the rest of the day, leaving all the books she had picked in the archive on Roman's desk.

She watched the rose tinted sky turn golden and then blue, her mind still wandering the shelves of the archive. Would she ever fully leave the archive? Nodin was tempted to lock herself in the archive and never leave, becoming a ghost of this world.

"Eat." Roman handed her a raspberry pastry, and a mug of steaming cocoa. Nodin nibbled at the sweet drink, the hot cocoa warming up her soul. "Let's sleep." Roman seemed to know that Nodin was grieving something much deeper than just herself. Roman didn't push her, settling down with her in his bed. Nodin sank into a deep sleep haunted for once by something other than the creature, deeply wishing for it to come back.

31

Nodin slept for two days, Roman by her side the whole time. Waking up on the second morning she felt more like her old self. She knew what she needed to heal the last broken pieces she had lost in the archive. "Morning, mea nox lux," Roman murmured into her hair. "Morning, meus rex tenebris," Nodin kissed Romans forehead.

"What would you like to do today?" Roman glanced at the pile of books she had yet to touch. "There is something I need to do," Nodin ran her fingers through her tangled hair. "Anything you need from me?" Roman started to gently tease the tangles from her hair.

"I would like for you to come with me." Nodin tilted her head back as Roman brushed through her hair. "I would love to join you." It took Roman almost an hour till he could smoothly run a brush through her hair.

They dressed warmly, heading down for breakfast in comfortable silence. Without a word, Nodin walked through the school's greenhouse Roman following her, watching her in awe as she bounced through the winding paths.

Nodin stopped in the middle of the greenhouse in front of a large black lotus tree, its white blooms hanging down. As Nodin approached the tree one of its large limbs bent down to greet her. Roman stood in shock watching the tree move by itself. Nodin closed her eyes, feeling the heartbeat of the tree's soul ringing through her. A single leaf from the tree drifted down into Nodin's waiting hand.

As the leaf touched Nodin's palm the bright green leached from the leaf, turning gray then in a blink it turned bright white silver. Glittering in her palm, reflecting the green oasis around them. Nodin turned back to Roman with a sad smile, reaching out her other hand for his. He held on to her hand tightly. Nodin brought the leaf to her lips, kissing the leaf, her prayer transferring to the leaf.

The leaf started to glow with starlight sinking into the soft skin of her lips. The world around them turned dark, a spiraling dark black-brown fog dancing around the void they were floating in. Before their eyes could adjust to the darkness that tried to tempt them to stay, a strong wind slammed into them. Nodin lost her grip on Roman's hand as the hit the hard ground.

Nodin pushed herself off the ground: gone was the snow, replaced by sharp chips of stone. Brushing off the shards of stone that clung to her hands, she looked around for Roman. He mirrored her, knocked to the ground, brushing himself off. Nodin looked out from the plateau; they stood in the heart of a mountain range, spread out before them. Nodin smiled as the fresh air opened up her lungs, the power of mountains thundering in her veins.

A narrow path was carved into the side of the mountain, leading up into the peak of the mountain. "Where are we?" Roman asked, following her down the path. "Very far away," Nodin gave him a non-answer. They hiked up the mountain in silence, despite the altitude, a comfortable cool temperature, and the wind dancing around them. It was not long till Nodin reached the top of the mountain, a spattering of grass growing from the rocks.

A single tree grew from the rocks, its twisted roots twisting up into the trunk. Its long branches reached out over the mountain top. Something about the tree spoke of its power, radiating aged wisdom. Compared to the magic of the sea dragon's cave and the beauty of the crystal cave it was merely an old tree, its deceit whispered on the wind.

Roman panted beside her, the grass thickening under their feet as they approached the tree, tufts of blue-green grass brushing their knees. Nodin stopped beneath the branches of the tree looking up at it. "This is the Wishing Tree." Nodin explained, "one of the three pillar trees. The tree of life, the tree of souls, and the tree of wishes." Nodin ran her fingers over the tree's thick bark.

"It is said that the three trees create the weave by intertwining their roots." Nodin dropped her fingers from the bark. "Why is one of the branches dead?" Roman looked at the blackened leaves, the wood bleached white. "It's the damage to the weave," Nodin smiled sadly at the branch. "What's killing it?" Roman reached out a hand towards the branch. Nodin snatched his hand back from the branch. "Mortal casting," Nodin whispered.

Roman was silent as he stared down at his hands. "I'm sorry." Roman looked up at her. Her heart broke a little for the man who grew up learning the very thing that was destroying the world around them, she could hardly blame him for the damage down years before his birth. *He is still part of the problem.* "The wishing tree is magic itself." Nodin turned back to the tree. "The tree of life is self-explanatory, and the tree of souls is the keeper of everyone's past."

"I thought the trees were just part of the elven belief system, not that they were physical trees." Roman scrunched his face recalling everything he had read on the trees. "Ready?" Nodin smiled brightly at him, the first full smile he had seen since the archive. Nodin pressed her hand to the bark of the tree, a deep tug in her chest was all the warning she got as the bark started to grow over her hand.

Roman placed his hand next to hers, gasping. Nodin tumbled forward, her body pitching into, and then through the tree. Nodin looked over at Roman who scanned the space around them. The void. *Welcome home.* A long root wrapped around each of their waists and disappeared into the darkness.

"Welcome, child," the light voice echoed around them. The tree's voice rang through her head and around the void. "What is it that you seek?" the tree asked her. "An answer," she replied to the tree, her lips unmoving. "Why did the archive pick us?"

Nodin waited for the tree's response.

"For the same reason it picked your parents. The doors of the archive are carved from a branch gifted by the tree of souls." Nodin had not expected a straight answer from the tree but she was unsure of what to do with the answer it had given her. "He asked if there was a way to learn elven casting so that mortals could stop damaging the weave." Nodin felt the tree looking at Roman who looked bewildered to be talking to a tree in his mind.

Without another word, the root pulled them back through the void and back to their bodies. "Why don't we ask the tree how to solve all our problems?" Roman hadn't lost the bewilderment in his eyes. "Because to find the tree you have to ask its permission, its not here to solve our problems," Nodin explained. "Not even when our problems are killing it?" Roman couldn't see the bigger picture.

Nodin couldn't either. "The tree gives what it wants," was the only answer Nodin had for him. "The tree didn't answer my question," Roman admitted to her. "It only said that a lock needs a key." Roman shook his head. "The tree did answer your question, even if you don't understand its answer."

"Do not stress Roman, even the greatest elven minds do not understand the answers the tree gives them for many years." Nodin kissed his cheek, smiling at his mind spinning behind his eyes. "You should be more worried when you understand the tree's answer."

"How do we get home?" Roman looked out over the mountains that surrounded them, as far as the eye could see peaks rose into the sky. "We walk." Nodin smiled at him. "You are joking right?" Roman watched her in horror as she started to walk down the mountain. "Right?" he yelped as he followed her.

Nodin stopped just several paces down the path, pointing to a small pond down the path. "It's a pond," Roman stated matter-of-factly. "It's our way home." Nodin danced her way towards the pool, unencumbered by her lack of understanding of her answer from the tree. As the pair approached the pool it shone with the light of the sun, casting an orange aura around it.

Nodin bent down, scooping up some of the golden liquid into her palms. Bringing it over to Roman, her hands cast a bright glow over her face. Letting the water run off her hands and into his, the water was warm to the touch sparking and dancing with sunlight.

"It's stunning." Roman watched the water run off his hand, dripping to the floor. "How does this get us home?" Nodin winked at him, grabbing the front of his jacket, and pulled him off his feet and into the water. They both tumbled into the water, the warmth wrapping them in a hug before they slammed into the soft familiar scent of Roman's bed. Nodin was wrapped in Roman's protective arms, he felt his chest vibrating as his laugh filled the room. He let her go running his hand over his dry clothing. "That was amazing."

32

Nodin was curled up in Roman's bed, his roommates had returned to the school only hours before. Nodin listened as they ribbed him for cleaning the whole dorm. "That's settled, Roman's the new cleaning bitch!" Sullan laughed, his voice floating through the door and into Nodin's ears. "Then next time do a shit job at it!" Only parts of the conversation were reaching her ears which made it all the funnier.

It was late by the time the two of them were drifting off to sleep in a post-orgasm haze, tangled in the blankets together, huddled as close as they could, stealing each other's body heat -the frozen air leaking into the room from around the window. Classes started tomorrow and all the students had returned to the school -Nodin silently mourned their relationship, it was getting stuffed back in a small box hidden under the bed.

Nodin scrambled up from the stone floor. Her knees scraped over the rough stone warm blood seeping into her tights. Her shoes scuffed up the floor as she fought to regain balance as she flung herself along the hall. Tripping around a corner she fell into the entrance hall, the sound of the claws on stone echoing around the large space.

Hurtling through the entrance hall towards the dining hall Nodin stretched out her legs to eat up the distance. Fighting her screaming muscles to keep going. She felt the eyes of the creature on her back as she scrambled away from it. The sound of its claws sent shivers down her spine and strength to her muscles.

Nodin slammed her body against a door in the back of the dining hall, it gave way under her, releasing her into a small dark hallway. Barreling down the hall Nodin panted, the air burning her lungs. The maze of halls spat her out into a small classroom, nothing more than a room with twenty small tables and chairs in front of a large desk.

Nodin panicked, trapped in a dead end, she shoved the table out of her way -storming through the room. She spotted the door tucked behind the large desk just as the creature made it to the door she had entered. Darting through the door, slamming it closed behind her, she bolted as fast as her feet could take her.

While the halls and rooms looked like the schools, the layout was incorrect, this hall opened up into the library, the towers of books looming over her watching her fight for her life. Nodin ran past the shelves of books, the creature running right through the shelves, knocking them over. Send books scattering to the floor and shards of wood through the air.

Nodin's knees gave out from under her slamming her body into the floor of the library. The wind knocked out of her lungs -she choked *as she tried to crawl along the ground away from the creature.*

Nodin gasped air filling her lungs, her eyes flying open with a jolt. Roman shook her body one more time. Her knees bruising before their eyes. The dark room welcomed her back, her whole body burned, covered in sweat. Roman's grip on her loosened, worry etched into his features. "Mea nox lux! Holy fuck. Are you okay?" Roman gripped her tightly to his chest, breathing deeply into her hair.

Nodin didn't answer him, her mind still running on pure panic. "You are safe," he whispered, brushing her hair with his hand and cupping the back of her neck with his palm.

"Nightmare," Nodin breathed, finally able to form wards. "What about?" Nodin looked at him through the dark, and searched his face. "I am haunted by a void beast," Nodin finally settled on the truth. She trusted him with her deepest secret. It was time to trust him with her darkest. "A void beast?" Roman searched his memory for what she was talking about coming up with only children's tales. "How?" Roman had started to question everything he knew, that the myths and tales he had filed away as untrue were far from it.

"My parents…"

33

"My father was an elf and my mother a mortal." Nodin was lost in her memory, giving voice to the flashback that danced behind her eyes.

They lived in hiding from the mortal world and were ostracized by the elven world. My father taught me how to use the weave, taught me the elven principles and way of life from a very young age. We were happy, I knew nothing of the struggles of the world. Of the divide of my people. That all changed when I was about six. I had found a deer in the field behind our house, it had died from a gunshot to the shoulder, probably dragging itself away from the mortals until its body finally gave out on it in our wildflower field.

I was so young, while I knew what death was, the elves don't shy away from it -nor from teaching their young about it- I did not truly understand it. I was so sad finding that deer. I brought it back, I did not know the consequence of my actions. I didn't know. I didn't know what I was doing was wrong, I just wanted to help the poor deer. Its fur was all matted with blood, but I could tell it was beautiful. Its huge brown eyes stared right through me. I brought it back to life with my small hands, it was so easy. Too easy.

Bringing back the deer ripped a hole in the weave. Bringing back its soul from the tree of souls tore a hole in the weave. It never truly came back, anyway. It was a monstrous grotesque husk of its former self. I don't know what happened to the deer, it bolted away from me towards the forest, black sludge poring from its eyes. It was the last thing I saw before I fell into the hole in the weave.

Right into the void. I hadn't noticed the hole that was behind me till it had swallowed me. It was so cold. I don't know how long I was in the void. By the time my parents found me a void beast had found me first, and was dragging me down deeper into the void. My mother pulled me out of the void, she got me out but she didn't follow me out. She had traded places with me.

My father tried to close the hole I had created, but the void beast was climbing through the hole. It forced its way through the hole and into our realm. Split between closing the hole and keeping the void beast away from me, my father struggled to save us both.

The void swallowed him, it thrashed out at him trying to close the hole. Dragging him down to join his wife, in a last-ditch effort he closed the hole after him. Locking the void beast in our realm with me.

"… haunting me ever since." Nodin blinked, clearing her mind of the fuzzy memories, the years had faded them, the panic of that day locking them in the depths of her mind. Roman took her face in his hands, wiping the stream of tears from her cheeks.

"Haunting you?" Roman wiped each new tear that rolled down

her cheeks. "It's in my dreams, sometimes I see it in mirrors or hear it, but I haven't seen it since I was six," Nodin explained, "but it's always been there, just out of sight."

34

Nodin stood in the doorway watching all the students bustle by. The two weeks over Yule had changed her. Not in any big way, but how she looked at the school had changed. She had opened up to Roman, she had someone in her corner who saw all of her -all her teeth and wasn't scared. *Just because he isn't scared of your teeth doesn't mean he isn't scared of your bite.*

With a heavy heart, she watched the small crowd that enclosed the heirs move through the entrance hall disappearing into the far hall toward their classes. The hours they had spent together hidden away in the folds of their memory.

Nodin dragged herself from her class feeling drained, the professors had been holding back all last semester and they had stepped it up in this one. They were brutal in their teaching. *Goodbye, arm floaties.* Drifting through the crowd headed to the dining hall, Nodin had agreed to meet her friends there for lunch, she got stuck behind an older couple, the crowd not letting her pass by them.

They weren't any faculty or professors she had seen before at the school. Her stomach twisted as she looked at the back of

148

their heads, something familiar about their clothes that she could not place.

Between the heads of the older couple she could see a woman about her age walking with them, slightly in front of them, she turned to talk to them every couple of paces. She had long white hair, a warm pink glow to her skin, and features plucked from a fairytale.

The crowd moved forward slowly, filling up the dining hall, the chatter bouncing off the ceiling. Nodin's heart stuttered as she glimpsed Roman through the crowd, he was leaning against a wall talking to the heirs, animated as he talked waving his hands through the air. Quietly she did admit to herself that they did look like a good group together, the heirs from the outside looked like a close-knit group of young men ready to take on the world together.

As she neared them she could overhear the older couple talking to the younger woman, about how she would love the school here. "Son!" the older man called out in greeting, smiling as he spread his arms wide. Roman stood up straight smiling as he hugged the older man, his father.

Nodin scampered to the other side of the dining hall door, tucking herself in a corner watching them. "We missed you," Roman's mother said, hugging her son. She seemed like a warm person who would bake you fresh cookies and listen to your problems as you ate half a batch in one sitting.

"Hello. Dearest fiancé." The young woman smiled, a cold chill biting at her face. Her sharp tone and calculating eyes did not match her pleasant features. She was looking right at Roman, and he wasn't correcting her. *His fiancé?* Nodin's heart stopped in her chest, the weave licking at her fingers responding to her raging emotions.

Panic slammed into her, roaring in her ears she missed what they were saying. Everything in her screamed. It couldn't be true? Right? Roman's gentle tone seeped into her mind. "Hello, Hester. What are you doing here?" *Hester.*

"I am now a student here, at your quaint little school." Hester smiled, a monster showing her teeth. "Hello, sister," Ivor greeted smiling, his light eyes just as cold as hers. "Brother." Nodin watched in horror at the scene unfolding in front of her. Roman was unaware of her presence, of her breaking heart just feet from him. What was she to him? Something fun to distract him while he was away from his fiancé? *A toy.*

Through the panic the rage started to boil through, hardening her face as it started to steam. She bared her teeth at the world turning to storm away from her broken heart scattered all over the floor. It was then that Roman looked up, spotting her across the room, his face dropping, eyes darting from her to Hester.

Nodin bolted, her feet flying over the ground and tearing through the space. She could hear the familiar sounds of Roman's footsteps behind her, it did not escape her the echo of her dream last night.

Nodin twisted and turned, flying through the crowd at an unnatural pace; she lost him in the crowd, and he was unable to keep up. Dipping into an empty hall, she let out a breath slouching against the wall, only then did she let her tears fall. *That is what you get for trusting others.* Letting out a strangled scream she whipped around slamming her fist into the stone wall. Pulling back her throbbing but unmarred hand little chunks of stone fell to the floor spider webs of cracks spanned over the wall.

Nodin sank to the floor, exhausted and numb, and sat with her head against the cold stone. Then she rose, dragging herself to class her mind in a haze. *He will not ruin you.*

II

Gone

The spark flickered and went out.

35

Nodin sat in silence with her friends watching her like a hawk. Despite the many hours since lunch, she was still numb. It had sunk deep into her bones, a bottomless pit in her chest. The scrape of a chair beside Nodin pulled her eyes from her food and to the angelic face of Hester. "Hello. I'm Hester." She bounced into the chair beside her smiling. "Hello. I'm Nodin." Nodin's face twitched as she looked at the woman before her.

Nodin went back to her food, spooning the coconut and pumpkin curry into her mouth. The silence dragged on as Hester nibbled on her ox and rabbit stew, the warm spice scent of her food wafting over Nodin. "So you are Roman's fiancé." Nodin looked over at her again, her small bowl of food, the way she dabbed at her lips with her napkin.

"Yes. I was at Haggards, but I transferred here to be closer to him," She smiled widely, her teeth too big for her face. Her smile never reached her cold eyes, the same eyes she shared with Ivor. *Bite her.* "That's amazing." Nodin choked on her words. "Hester! Over here!" Ivor called across the room waving her over to the heirs usual table. Roman sat next to

155

him staring at his food. He couldn't even look at her.

"Later." Hester flounced off towards her brother and fiancé. *Fiancé.* Nodin frowned at her back watching her white hair swish over her back. Her spoon scraped the bottom of her bowl with a screech. Scoping the last mouth full, Nodin watched Hester sit down next to Roman, leaning her head against his shoulder, her hand sliding up his chest.

Roman peeled her arm off him, whispering something to her quietly, and finally he looked up at her. He held Nodin's gaze across the room. While he was distracted, Hester had stood up standing behind him, sliding her hands into his hair.

Nodin stood so fast the chair skittered across the floor. Nodin broke eye contact with him, the lasting image of his fiancé with her hands in his hair stuck in her mind. Nodin fled the dining hall as fast as her feet could take her. Her heart split open in her chest, breaking through the wall of numb feelings. Anguish bubbled up her throat, choking her.

Feeling reckless Nodin jumped from the hall to the lake. Slowly she loosened the chains wrapped around her heart, the emotion spilling out of her in waves, tears scorching her face, large waves of raw weave rolling off of her smashing into the world around her. The top of the lake rippled with the force of the magic coming off of her.

Nodin collapsed on the beach as the magic that flowed from her ebbed. Something nagged at her senses despite the darkness in her mind. *You woke something up.* Nodin felt it, something in the lake was moving. Something big, and old.

A ripple on the surface of the lake, small a single ribbon running along the top of the lake. Then another. A large bubble broke the surface. Slowly a head rose from the lake, the dark blue scales framed by glowing red eyes. Water streamed off its head as it blinked at her. A deep sea wyrm had been sleeping in the lake.

Nodin held her breath as it took her in, temperamental beasts they were, reflecting the ever-changing moods of the ocean. What it was doing in a lake was beyond her. She dipped her head, turning it slightly to the left, showing the sign of respect shared between members of its species.

"You woke me." Its deep voice echoed in her head. "I didn't mean to. I did not realize you were here," Nodin answered, still keeping her head down. "You have been here before, you have stirred me before." Nodin thought back, through her mind. Had she? "I apologize."

"Do not, child. You walk this path just like I." The deep sea wyrm's voice had a nostalgic edge. "I did not know a lake could serve as your respite." Nodin gingerly raised her head by several inches, taking in the dragon's thick neck. "I was born here, before the time the mortals built their huts in the forest." Nodin would not call the school a hut, but she supposed to the wyrm it was. What were the chances that this lake housed two dragons?

"There is a reason they built that wretched thing here, the

weave here is strong. This place is one of many anchors." Nodin was familiar with anchors, elves often settled near them, as they were strong older sections of the weave that kept it going, like a heart with its veins.

"I shall rest soundly knowing you walk this forest." Slowly the deep sea wyrm sank back below the surface. Nodin watched the water settle to its calm mirrored surface. Between the two dragons, the archive, the school, and the anchor this forest was seeped in more history than anyone knew. No wonder the students thought this lake was dangerous, she was sure many a meddling student had woken up the wyrm and paid the price, completely unaware of the creature below.

Nodin wasn't alone for long, the far-off sound of footsteps flying through the forest met her ears. The rhythm was as familiar to her as her heart beat. Taking in a deep breath, she was gone long before Roman made it out of the trees.

36

Nodin sat in her bed, in the dark, wrapped tightly in her blankets. The emotions were still fighting within her, but the violent warring had calmed down. Nodin pulled open the draw in her night stand, pulling out the warm bundle of paper. It had been a while since she had looked at them. The letters she and Roman had exchanged all that time ago. It felt like years had passed since things between them had been so simple.

She slipped the green ribbon from the letters, spreading them out on the bed before her. How had she not known? Not seen? He had been lying to her this whole time and she had trusted him. *Trust is a dangerous gift.* And she had given it to the wrong person. What was she to him? Nothing? Something cute to entertain him?

Nodin got lost reading the letters from a simpler time, when she didn't know who her pen pal was. When no one knew her secret. When she had not found the archive. When it was just surviving school, and escaping to the peaceful lake. It was late into the night when a soft knock tapped on her door. She looked up to watch the door slowly swing open.

Nodin could smell the scent of waterlilies and musk floating through the door, the outline of Roman standing in her door frame, nothing more than a darker black than the night around him. "Nodin." Gone was the nickname. "Roman." Neither of them moved. "Can we talk?" Roman stepped into her room. "What is there to say? You used me. You have a fiancé," Nodin's words bit into the air at him. "You are a language I am no longer fluent in, but still remember how to read," Nodin let the tears fall in the darkness, "…let me forget."

Roman was silent, as he took a step back. "No! I will not let you forget. Technically you are right, but please let me explain." Roman stood his ground. Something in Roman's tone stopped her, maybe she hadn't completely forgotten the language that was him. Roman took her silence as consent. "I never used you. I love you. Hester… Hester is… our parent's planned our wedding years ago. I was eight! I don't want to marry her. I don't even like her. She was my friend when we were children, she also hated our parents' arrangement. In the last five years she has changed, she switched sides on the marriage. I want out!" Roman stood bare, raw before her.

"What does that mean for us?" Nodin could not let herself hope. "It changes nothing." Nodin's heart stuttered in her chest, broken before it had come back to life. Her face hardened along with her heart. "So we stay a secret and the whole school believes you're engaged as she continues to fawn all over you?" Nodin snapped at him, not caring if she drew blood. "Well…" Roman faltered, taken aback by her tone.

"No! You never make room for me. Over and over I am hurt to make room for you!" Nodin yelled at him, snarling her teeth. *Bite him, let him feel your pain.* "I'm sorry." Roman sounded hollow. "You are sorry?! That's not enough!" Nodin was getting hysterical, she felt it in her throat. "Tell me! Tell me anything I can do to show you that you are everything to me!" Roman roared back at her. Nodin looked at him. Was he asking her to fix the problem he made?

"I would tear down heaven and lift up hell and make you Queen of both." Roman walked towards her, wrapping his arms around her. "I want something that says you're mine," Nodin said into Roman's chest. "What?" Roman tried to pull back from her. "I don't know," Nodin muttered, feeling deflated. "I have an idea." Roman pulled at the thin chain that was tucked into Nodin's clothing. Pulling the necklace off of her he looped it around his neck clasping it. The silver pendant flashed at her in the light.

"You can not lose that." Nodin watched the pendant slip under his shirt. The outline of the circle visible through the material. It was two vines wrapping around each other forming a circle, two ivy vines cast in silver, locked into time forever. "I won't lose it," Roman promised. Nodin placed her hand on his chest over the pendant. It had been her mother's, her father had given it to her at their wedding. Her mother had worn it everyday, except for the day she had died.

"I'm yours." Roman pulled her hand to his lips, kissing her knuckles. "We will find a way." He promised to himself, whispered against her hand. "Don't make promises you can't keep," Nodin whispered back. She felt Roman's eyes on her. "I am keeping this promise, I will do everything to make this work." Roman gripped her hand, running his other hand over her cheek.

Nodin rested her head against Roman's chest, listening to his heart hammering under his skin. "Please forgive me?" Roman nuzzled his face into her wild hair. "I forgive you." Nodin wasn't sure she could do this. "I make no promises this will work."

"Just give me the chance," Roman pleaded. Nodin nodded, flipping her fingers through the weave, the candles in the room sparking to life.

37

In the days that followed, Nodin and Roman could not find time to spend with each other. Watching Hester throw herself at Roman was painful, she took advantage of every opportunity to place her hands on him. To his credit, Roman batted her hands away and kept wearing Nodin's necklace. As the days apart stretched on Hester picked up on Roman watching Nodin. Nodin watched Hester plant herself between them, blocking his view of her.

Nodin was tempted to send her bowl of frozen sorbet flying into her face, her dislike of Roman's fiancé growing day by day. While the majority of the school had been indifferent to her, minus the leering comments by Ivor, that had changed since Hester's arrival. It seemed Hester had thrown herself into a smear campaign instead of her studies. Nodin's friends had defensively stuck by her side, their names being smeared in mud for their association.

"Bullying is definitely against the school rules." Ascelin glared at Hester's blonde head. "You think the school will hold her to the same rules?" Odette raised her eyebrows at Ascelin. She had a point, she was the child of one of the current ruling chairs

-her brother being an heir. "You are right," Nodin chipped in. "Plus what proof do I have that it's her?" Ascelin looked at her.

"True, but it is her, we know it is." Willow added. "It's not right," Ascelin wrinkled her face. "We could…" Ascelin started. "Try anything no matter how just it is and you will be the one getting in trouble," Willow warned, pointing at Ascelin and then at Nodin. Both women nodded fervently at her.

Leaving breakfast with her friends flanking her did not stop the less-than-subtle remarks, and dirty looks she got walking the halls. Nodin tried to ignore the whispers that followed her down the hall. "Ms. Merle!" Nodin turned around to see her history of casting Professor striding towards her down the hall. "Yes?" Nodin looked up at him, he was a tall man with a stern face, his dark hair sprinkled with gray.

"Can we talk?" Though the words were supposed to sound like a question, they were not, they were a demand. Glancing back at her confused friends Nodin followed the professor back to his office. She searched the far corners of her mind as to why he needed to talk to her, she had missed an assignment, her grades were good but not great, and she hadn't broken any school rules -at least not any he would know about.

"Have a seat." Professor Bardo sank into his chair behind his desk. "May I ask what this is about?" Nodin perched on the edge of the wooden chair. "Well, while you are not necessarily failing my class it has come to my attention that you aren't doing so well in your other classes. I just wanted you to know that your grades in my class will not keep you here. And if your grades in your other classes don't improve, I will have to reevaluate your grades in mine." The professor stared at her, his elbows resting on his desk.

"I... didn't think my grades in my other classes were bad..." Nodin's mind stuttered, shocked, she had not been expecting that. Dropping her grade in one class because she wasn't performing in another. *Idiot.* "You didn't think your grades were bad?" Professor glared at her. "You are failing them." Nodin knew she wasn't failing a single class, her grades weren't the top in her class but she was nowhere near failing.

"I'm not. Have you talked to my other professors?" Nodin sat up straighter in her seat matching the professor's glare. "No, but..." Professor Bardo started, but Nodin cut him off. "Where did you hear that I am failing?"

"It does not matter," the professor shoot back in his chair. "No it does, because if you dragged me in here to threaten to drop my grade based on nothing but rumors then yes, it matters," Nodin snarled at him, standing up and leaning forward. Professor Bardo leaned back, staying quiet.

"Now unless my grades, based on my work, in your class, are substandard then I will be leaving." Nodin turned and stormed out of the room.

As she left the office she spotted Hester leaning against the far wall, chatting with her friends, all laughing. She turned to her smiling, a wicked gleam in her eye. She looked like a doll, her clothes crisp, she had accessorized her school uniform just within the guidelines, her hair perfect. Everything about her was prim and proper, her grades perfect.

The right bloodline from a powerful family, the skills in casting to back it up, everything about her was perfect. Nodin ground her teeth, brushing her wrinkled skirt flat. "Morning, Nodin." Hester smiled, her voice so sickly sweet it was nothing but poisonous.

"Morning, Hester," Nodin ground out. "You know I could help you study if you need help." Hester pointed to Professor Bardo's door, "He only pulls students into his office if they are failing. I wouldn't want to see you fail." Hester's friends snickered at her. "No, I am good Hester, I'm not failing he was wrong. He was listening to gossip." Nodin held her head high, smiled at her and walked away.

~

Her professors had kept a closer eye on her all through her classes all week, just waiting to see the proof that she was a failure. That they too had listened to Hester over their own thoughts of her. The sway she had over the whole school. *If only she knew who she was dealing with.* Nodin sulked into her bowl of fruit, her toast getting cold in her hand.

"She graduates this year," Ascelin pointed out, staring at the vapid queen bee. "Then she can't mess with your schooling." Ascelin tried to smile convincingly. "I just have to make it through this one," Nodin pointed out. "Yeah." Ascelin sounded a little deflated.

Nodin looked up from her food and glanced around the room. Everyone was looking at her. The whispering she had been trying to block out filtered back to her. Whispers how she shouldn't have been allowed in the school, how she was failing, speculating on how she was still here. What professor she had slept with to stay at the school? If she was blackmailing the school to keep her and what it was.

Nodin settled into her seat, her nerves fried, this was the first time she had Professor Bardo's class since he had pulled her into his office. Her classmates spared her the stress of openly gossiping about her in the classroom, but it did not spare her from their eyes. Ranging from curiosity to outright hatred painted the eyes of her classmates. The professor walked into class, clapping his hands bringing the class's attention away from Nodin.

"Due to a recent discussion with one of your peers, I feel I have to remind you that insinuating that a professor is evaluating you on anything but your grades is peevish and childish and will not be tolerated," Professor Bardo kept his eyes trained on Nodin through his whole speech. Nodin glared at the professor, she had been short with him but she had not been peevish, however, the professor felt the need to publicly shame her due to his own fragile ego.

Ascelin turned to Nodin and mouthed 'what?' at her. Nodin shook her head, mouthing 'later'. The class went smoothly after the rough start. As the class packed up, Ascelin leaned over her desk leaning on her elbows. "What was that about?" Nodin packed up her bag not looking at Nodin.

"He basically informed me that he had heard rumors that I was failing all my classes and before checking if I was actually failing threatened to fail me in this class if I didn't improve my grades in my other classes, and I called his bullshit." Nodin gave Ascelin a grim smile, giving her a knowing look. Ascelin sat in her chair gaping at her. "Really?" Ascelin was gobsmacked. "Ass," Willow added before they left for their next class.

38

Nodin tucked her chin down, marching from her first class to her second one, whispers following her down the hall. Nodin spun backward as a body collided with her, pinwheeling her arms back trying to catch her falling body. Nodin slammed into the ground violently, jarring her back. "Can't even walk properly," the person snarled at her before walking away, leaving her alone on the ground.

"Why do you even go to class at this point!" someone yelled at her down the hall. "She's failing," another person whispered to her friend as they rushed past. "Do everyone a favor and leave!" Ivor hollered at her, smirking across the hall at her.

Nodin pulled herself from the floor, her elbow stinging, the warmth of her blood dripping down her arm. Cupping her arm to her body, Nodin fled to the nearest woman's washroom. Racing to the sink Nodin peeled back her sleeve to survey the damage. Bruised to high heaven but only a shallow gash in her skin. Flipping on the tap Nodin let the cold water run over her angry skin.

"How are you?" The poisonously sweet voice of Hester popped

169

up right beside her. Hester had braided her hair into two thick braids pinned at the end with a pale pink bow. Her lips matched the color of the bows, and she had on a pink silk neck scarf tightly wound around her throat. "Oh sorry. I'm ok," Nodin started, turning to face her.

Hester stepped closer to her, tipping her head to the side. "Bet you thought you were special with all that attention from Roman, huh?" Hester made a small hiccup sound, and wrinkled her nose, Nodin supposed it may have been cute from anyone else, but on Hester, it looked downright psychotic.

"What?" Nodin frowned at her. Hester looked at her blankly, her large eyes going a bit bug-eyed in her face. "But you aren't special." Hester's hand darted out, flipping the tap all the way open, before quickly shutting it back off. The water hit the side of the basin and splashed up Nodin, soaking the left side of her skirt and dripping down her tights. "Oops," Hester said with a smile and skipped out of the washroom humming. *Bitch.*

Nodin slammed her palms down on the rim of the skin, glaring at her reflection. Nodin grabbed at some towels dabbing at her clothes. There was nothing she could do about her skirt; it had absorbed most of the water, but she got most of the water out of her tights. The cloth of her tights was still slightly damp, making her flesh goose-pimpled under the cold fabric.

Nodin straightened herself up, she took one last look in the mirror, the woman who stared back at her was a shell of the soul it housed. Dark circles decorated her face, a small splash of blood on her elbow, half of her skirt wet, and her hair had freed itself from the bun escaping in every direction.

Nodin was late to class, slipping in the door and hiding in the shadows in the back. Despite her better judgment, she tugged lightly at the weave to hide her arrival, making it so her professor didn't think anything it.

Nodin smiled to herself. This professor had boasted at length about their skill manipulating the raw magic as they put it, but had not caught on to Nodin's blatant casting of the weave right under their nose. Talented raw caster her ass. *Abomination of magic. How can you even call that casting?*

39

Nodin's body hurt, the stone beneath her digging into her flesh. Nodin fought against her eyelids, unable to lift them. Nodin flexed her fingers along the cold stone, her fingers tinged numbly fumbling over the stone. Nodin's head spun, the world dipping and falling around her. Nodin's stomach lurched, her hand flying to her mouth.

Panic gripped her chest, Nodin grasped at the weave, finding it beating steadily under her grasp. Nodin's body was suddenly thrown forward, bile clawing up her throat and into her mouth. Nodin choked, on the bile gasping for air. Her eyes blinked open, her mind unable to decipher the blurry mess her eyes saw. Her head pounded with a dull throb followed by a sharp throb. The hands on her biceps pulled her to a sitting position. "Are you okay?" the voice floated through deep thick water echoing around her head.

The fuzzy face of a round older woman peered at her, her face pinched in concern. Dressed in a thick nightgown and robe, the professor's strong grip on her arms grounded Nodin. Nodin's face pinched in the pain assaulting her head, she waved her hands in the air.

"Yeah." She tried to pull her arms from the professor's grip. Freeing herself from the fingers of the professor, Nodin tumbled to the ground again, the cold stone kissing her cheek. Nodin hissed in pain pushing her body up from the floor. "Here." The professor leaned her against the wall, and the world slowly stopped spinning.

"What happened?" the soft voice of the professor coaxed her to spill every little detail of all her problems over the last month. "I don't know." Nodin ran her hand over her face, closing her eyes, banishing the memories from her mind. She did know. *Naughty liar.* "Nodin." Her name echoed around the halls, followed by heavy running footsteps. Roman came flying down the hall in all abandon. Roman collapsed next to the professor, his knees slamming into the stone. He leaned forward scanning her face and body, taking in the wreck before him.

"Get checked out by the school medic," the professor instructed her firmly. "I trust you will make sure she gets there, Mr. Van'Hight." The professor gave him a strong stare, warning of eternal torment if he failed her. "Of course." Roman got to his feet, crouching before her. Nodin protested profusely as he scooped her up in his arms, carrying her down the hall.

"Stop whining. And let me enjoy the feeling of you in my arms," Roman warned her, tightening his grip on her. The whole trip to the infirmary Roman did not ask her what happened. "I have missed you," Roman whispered before marching through the doors of the infirmary.

"What is going on?" the thin willowy woman asked as she skittered from her desk. Her face was a deep tan, she wore her deeply wrinkled skin with pride. Her thin veiny hands were warm and strong as she helped Roman place Nodin in a bed.

Nodin felt the pain in her head ease as the woman started to cast spell after spell on her, rapidly firing questions at Roman -who answered as best he could. "How are you feeling, dear?" The stern tone she had used with Roman eased into a warm whisper. "Better," Nodin smiled at the older lady.

"I have to warn you, I will have to file a report to the school of this incident. As you can not explain how you got these injuries and they are consistent with the injuries one would receive in a fight." She clasped her hands in front of her waiting for Nodin to slip the truth. "I don't know what happened, I wouldn't ever start a fight with anyone. I don't want to get in trouble." Nodin peered up at the woman. *Would start a fight, wouldn't lose a fight I started.*

"By no means would my report insinuate that you are at fault, but I do have to file the report." She walked off to her desk. "You may go. If you don't feel well in the next three days, please come back." She smiled at the two of them before sitting down at her desk. They had been dismissed. Nodin slid off the bed and started to leave -Roman hot on her heels.

"What time is it?" Nodin peered through the empty halls. "Past ten." Roman slipped his hand into hers.

40

Nodin escaped the school after classes ended, passing by the dining hall to pack up a dinner for herself before heading to the lake. Once again she found sanctuary in the isolated lake. Settled on the edge of the lake, she gazed out over the vast surface, contemplating its size.

Nodin frowned at the lake, getting up and darting to the edge. Grasping some of the water with the weave, she formed narrow stairs from the liquid, stepping up them till she had an overview of the forest. The school rising before her in the distance perched like a vulture on the grassy hill, turning to the ocean of forest behind her she mentally mapped out the depths. Taking into account all the underwater caves, and tunnels that she had personally explored let alone all the ones she hadn't yet.

The lake had a significant underground stretch, and by her estimation it ran under the majority of the forest -if not all of it. Nodin looked out over the trees, the outer edge disappearing into the distance. Off in the distance she could see another lake, or more accurately another place the lake joined the surface.

Once again she marveled at the sheer amount of magic the mortals didn't know was right under their noses. Letting the water of the lake drop, falling through the air to rejoin the lake. Nodin plummeted through the air landing on the surface of the water without a splash. "Nodin," Roman called from the edge of the forest. Skipping across the beach towards him, she threw herself into his arms.

He gripped her with one arm, swinging her around through the air. Pressing a less-than-gentle kiss to her lips. "I got you something." In his other hand sat a plain white cardboard box. Nodin took the box from him, flipping open the flimsy lid.

Twelve chocolate-coated strawberries sat in a circle, they were dusted with flecks of gold. Nodin picked up one of the plumb fruits, taking a generous bite, the sweet flavor of the fruit sprang into her mouth cut by the dark chocolate. They may have been some of the sweetest, and juiciest strawberries she had ever eaten. "They are amazing." Nodin's lips dripped with the red juice, she licked them clean offering the box to Roman. He took one of the chocolates, and started walking towards the beach.

Nodin and Roman spent their first evening together in a while watching the wildlife around them, eating the chocolate covered strawberries. As the sun set, they watched a young hippocampus swimming in the shallows of the lake, watched over by its mother dwelling in the depths of the lake.

Nodin and Roman laughed with the small creature as it splashed about in the water. Watching the carefree creature enjoy the world it had been born into chased the dark thoughts from Nodin's thoughts away. "Spend the night with me," Roman whispered into her ear as the darkness wrapped them in its familiar arms.

~

Love drunk on each other's lips, Nodin and Roman snuck through the school's empty halls, Nodin had wrapped them in a blanket of shadows. They fought giggles as they stumbled hand in hand towards Roman's dorm. Nodin released their blanket of shadows as they made it into the hall before Roman's dorm. They walked carefully, watching to see if anyone left their dorms. Something caught Nodin's eye, just the slight flash of something not there. She stopped and looked into the mirror hanging on the wall. *So many mirrors.*

"Wait. I saw something." Nodin stared into the mirror, and there it was again. The familiar claws of the void beast clutching to the corner of the mirror. Nodin jumped back, her feet scrambled on the stone as Nodin backed away from the glass of the mirror, slowly the void beast slunk into frame. Its beady eyes smiled at her.

"Let's go." Nodin grasped Roman's hand fleeing down the hall pulling Roman behind her. "What was that?" Roman asked, confused at Nodin's frantic footsteps. "My void beast," Nodin panted, looking behind her. Roman's face drained of color looking back down the hall as if would see the beast coming after them.

Roman pulled her through the door, and into this room, locking the door behind them. *As if the door would stop anything.* "Distract me," Nodin whispered into the dark room. Roman's hands found her face, cupping her jaw in his palms.

His hungry lips nipped at her lips, dragging his warm tongue over her teeth. Without breaking his lips from hers, he ran his curious hands down her body. Roman's hungry hands pulled each piece of clothing off of her body.

Roman hiked Nodin up his body, carrying her to his bed. Roman smirked at her as he hooked her knees over his shoulders. Crossing her ankles behind Roman's head, Nodin moaned as Roman's mouth met her cunt. Nodin clamped her thighs around Roman's head as his fingers dug into the flesh of her hips.

Nodin lifted her hips slightly, allowing Roman a better angle, his tongue sinking deeper into her core. Nodin's fingers gripped the bed sheets, her thighs twitching around Roman's head as her orgasm built in her core. Pleasure coursed through her veins, soaking Roman's face, all the muscles in her body relaxed as the waves of her orgasm crested over her.

Licking his lips clean, Roman sprawled on the bed beside her. Nodin pulled her orgasm hazed body up and over Roman's, settling down on his lap. Nodin's smile promised all the wicked she had planned for the night.

41

Nodin walked down to the entrance hall wrapped up in her head, and a small tug ran up her spine, the weave shifting and swirling around her. Bringing her focus to the present, another tug on the weave sent pins and needles up her spine.

Nodin's eyes landed on a pair of familiar ones, ones she had spent many nights looking into. Drifting to the matching cold eyes of the Daunte siblings. The heirs stood in the doorway of the dining hall, Hester standing beside Roman. Hester watched as Nodin got closer, smiling at her. *Fangless bitch.* "I love you, fiancé," Hester announced loudly, stepping closer to Roman. Hester stood on her tiptoes, pressing her lips to Roman's, the whole room watching -unaware of the pain raging in Nodin's chest. To the onlookers it was nothing more than the love of one of their future leaders, lapping it up like thirsty dogs.

"What are you looking at, drop out?" Hester snarled before turning to face her, her triumph writing all over her features. The hall thundered with laughter, Hester's cackle rising above them all, her hand still on Roman's chest right on top of Nodin's necklace. Roman ripped her hand off his chest, pushing past her, almost knocking her to the ground.

"What the hell, Hester?" Roman paced towards Nodin - the whole room watching like hawks at the drama unfolding before them. Nodin stepped back from all the eyes. Cutting through the crowd backwards. Nodin stepped away from him. The crowd parted watching as Roman's long strides ate up the floor.

As Roman caught up with her Nodin looked into his eyes. The storm of emotions warring in them. "Nodin," he whispered just for her ears. Roman reached out, pulling on her clothing, gripping her close to his body, and clashed his lips on hers. His hand snaked around the back of her neck, his tongue teasing at her lips. Nodin's heart hammered through her, her body pressed against him the warmth of his skin soaking into her.

Suddenly, Nodin was ripped from Roman's hands, the sounds of the room coming back to her ears. Nodin was yanked by the back of her clothes, the finger nails of her assailant digging into the skin of her neck.

"You bitch! He's mine!" Hester screeched behind her. Nodin tried to pull herself free of Hester's grip, stumbling forward as Hester shoved her whole weight into Nodin. Hester's hand scratched through the air, snatching at Nodin's hair. Nodin tipped forward, sending herself to the ground to avoid Hester's claws. "Hester!" Roman shouted at her.

The crowd encircled the two women, watching as Hester came unglued. "He's mine!" Hester screeched at the top of her lungs, her eyes wide with desperation. Her normally pale skin was blotchy and red, her voice getting shriller the more she screamed. Hester started throwing wave after wave of scorching hot air at Nodin. Nodin gritted her teeth as each one slammed into her. The air started to catch on fire, wisps of fire floating through the air, little embers floating to the ground. Screaming at the top of her lungs Hester encased the two of them in a ring of fire, burning dark red on the stone fueled by Hester's rage.

Several of the onlookers went to step through the wall of flames, springing back their clothing alight, blisters forming on their skin. The fabric on Nodin's clothes singed -burning right off of her body. Let the heat boil her, let the sparks burn her all while not taking her eyes off of the deranged woman in front of her. Nodin could make out the distant sound of the crowd outside their fiery bubble cheering and laughing -many booing her name. Panting in rage Hester started to throw large swaths of raw weave at her, ripping and scratching at the weave around her.

42

Nodin braced for another wall of heat to slam into her; it never hit her, the weave twisted in front of her, someone throwing up a shield in front of her. The ring of flames around them gutted and died down to burning embers. Several of the professors had finally made it to the front of the crowd. Nodin's shoulders slumped, looking at Hester through the shield. She was livid, her arms pinned to her side, legs tied together, and gagged by ropes of invisible force.

Hester's glare was dark and twisted, small sparks bounced off of the shield as she continued to cast through her bonds. The professors were hurling questions at Hester, and the surrounding crowd, and finally at her. No one gave up the details of how the fight started, or how it had gotten so out of hand. "This is unacceptable," a red-faced professor yelled at everyone.

A dull boom echoed around the room, the shield in between the two women shuddering. Hester, through her bonds, had thrown a wave of raw magic at her. Hester had given up on breaking the school rules and now was working on breaking the law. The weave warped and screamed under Hester's touch.

Another wave hit the shield; large cracks formed in the surface, before returning to normal. It wouldn't take another hit. The weave around Hester started to fray. As she ripped another chunk of raw magic out of the weave, it split apart in little wisps, hurling the raw magic at her the shield buckled under the power.

Nodin gaped at everyone around her as they did nothing. Hester was trying to kill her in front of everyone and they were doing nothing. Nodin searched the crowd for Roman; surely he could do something to help her. She spotted him, pinned to Ivor's side by Vane and Remus. Finally, tears sprang from her eyes. *Fight back!*

Nodin turned to Hester as she ripped another chunk of the weave apart, and Nodin watched as a dark black hole spread through the weave behind her. The wave of raw magic slammed into her, sending her flying over the floor, head bouncing off the stone. Her head exploded in pain and blinding light. Nodin wrapped herself in the remaining unbroken weave, healing the damage to her body enough to stand up.

Slowly the hole in the weave drifted through the room, passing by Hester and into the middle of their circle. As the crowd of onlookers spotted the rip they started to panic, many of them running to the far side of the room -only a handful of students left the hall. Students from all classes gripped the hands of their peers, the fear bringing those who would have never talked to embrace.

An otherworldly scream came from the hole floating between

them. Void beasts. The panic left her body, as the tips of black claws gripped the edge of the hole. This beast was different from the last, its clawed hands had only three fingers, leading to thicker arms, moldy black fur coated its body, and tall thin ears twitched on the top of its head that led into a pig-like snout. Nodin wrinkled her nose at its appearance; how it managed to be uglier than the one haunting she did not know.

It's large body fell to the floor with a wet thud. It opened its snout, with two long tusks dripping with black blood, and snarled at the room. Nodin locked eyes with it, its ears twitching listening to her heartbeat. Letting out a snarling grunt as its body whipped around to face Hester, its right back leg dragging along the floor. Shaking it out, the muscles twitched before setting its weight on its leg, unharmed.

Hester threw a fistful of raw weave at it, angering it more and more with each hit. She was panicking, the rage she had turned to blind panic and she was lashing out. Before she had time to second guess herself Nodin grasped the weave and redirected the raw magic attacks Hester was blindly flinging. Hester screamed, collapsing to the ground, her body unable to keep up with her casting.

Nodin crafted a perfect shield, trapping the void beast and herself together. The thick walls of her shield simmering around her, the sounds of the panicking crowd fading to the background. The professors slammed their fists into her shield yelling at her to let the shield down. Ivor crouched down by his sister, dragging her limp crying form away from the beast.

Using the mortal's magic, well beyond the skill she should exhibit for her first year, Nodin fought the beast. Throwing objects at the beast, the irony didn't escape her as she sent a dagger of fire at the beast that she was using the same magic Hester had been using against her. She needed to be careful; the majority of casters could only cast in two aspects, a rare few branching into three, but if she had any chance at surviving this fight she needed to dip into the skills of every single one.

Nodin gritted her teeth. She was limiting herself to mortal casting she needed to abandon all other restraints -everyone else be damned. *Good girl.* The beast leapt into the air, flying over ten feet in the air. Nodin scrambled to launch a wall of burning air at the beast. It did nothing. The beast flew straight towards her.

Nodin crumpled to the ground under the weight of it, one hand crushing her chest, one wrapped around her neck. Nodin choked on the air in her lungs, and clawed at the creature's flesh. Its mouth snuffled at her, tusks digging into her skin. The putrid smell of the beast fanned over her, burnt rotten flesh and a sick, salty scent.

Nodin bared her teeth at the beast. *Use your fangs.* Screams pierced the shield, as a black shape jumped from one of the large mirrors hanging high on the wall. The beast that slipped through her shield like it was nothing, was her void beast. Now two of them. Nodin's beast leapt into the air, with its strong legs, and it landed on the back of the beast, choking it.

The two beasts forgot about Nodin and the mortals around

them. Tumbling and biting at each other, snapping and snarling at each other, ripping and tearing flesh. Black blood dripped and smeared all over the stone floor. Nodin pressed her back against her shield watching in horror at the two monstrosities fighting in front of her. Hoping that the two beasts tearing each other apart before her would not remember she was there.

Hester's void beast let out a blood-curdling screech, it echoed and bounced off the walls. It's neck was in the beaked jaw of Nodin's void beast bent at an unnatural angle. As the scream echoed around the hall the beast turned to an oil slick black sludge dripping from the beak of the void beast. As the black goo hit the ground it boiled and bubbled it evaporated into thick black smoke. Nodin blinked away the toxic black smoke from her eyes, watching the remaining void beast.

Nodin scrambled to stand up, unable to get her feet under her as the void beast walked towards her. The void beast looked down at her, its large beak clicking quietly. It dipped its head, its inky black skin stretched tight over its skull, its beak still coated in the black blood of the other void beast. Panic turned her muscles to stone.

Gently, the beast rested its head on her lap, a soft trilling purr emanating from deep in its chest. It closed its deep red eyes, laying out on the floor before her. *Hello, little monster.* The familiar echoed through her head. No. The little whispered voice in her mind was not her own, had never been her own. That was you? *Yes, child. I have always been with you.* But you haunted me? *Haunted? Protected? Nurtured? How different are they really?* The beast did not open its eyes. *Never let them clip your claws, little monster. You are far greater than you will ever know.*

The beast opened its eyes and looked up at her. It blinked several times before its skin started to slip off its body slowly turning to liquid, spreading all over her legs and the floor around her. The puddle of black blood started to steam curls of black mist rising into the air.

The smoke drifted through the air and landed on Nodin's skin, sinking into her. In moments, her body had absorbed the whole beast. The last tendril of smoke drifted over to the gaping hole in the weave, stitching the broken weave back together. The ugly scar in the weave was the only reminder of the day's events.

The shield around her shattered, falling to the ground in large shards, disappearing back into the weave. Nodin panted, the pain catching up with her body, the abuse it had endured; through the pain assaulting her body, Nodin felt the familiar warmth growing up her back, blooming at the top of her spine before disappearing.

Nodin's head spun, her vision going black, as she felt her body start to fall. She lost consciousness before her body hit the floor. A deep roar, screamed with abandon, ripped through her drowning mind as she fell, followed by familiar steps pounding towards her. And then nothing.

43

Nodin's eyes opened at the same time her mind came swimming back to her. The room she was in was cloaked in darkness, the odd shapes of unfamiliar furniture sticking out in the dark. It was silent, shy of the sound of soft breathing coming from somewhere beside her. Peering through the darkness, she studied the shape of the person curled up in the chair beside the bed she was sprawled out on.

Roman. He had slumped over in his chair, his head resting on the edge of her bed, right next to her knees. Her sore body protesting the movement she ran her fingers through his thick hair. Roman sat up with a start, looking around the room. "Nodin," he whispered, his voice hoarse.

"Hello." Nodin's voice was soft and a little gravelly. "Mea tenebris anima mea," Roman mumbled, gathering her up in his arms, rocking her against his chest. Roman the small lamp in the corner of the room on, the warm light illuminating the walls. "Can you help me to the mirror?" Nodin pointed to the plain body-length mirror that was attached to the back of the door.

Slowly, they shuffled across the room, till Nodin stood leaning against him in front of it. Turning her back to the glass she tugged up the hem of her thin hospital shirt to look at her back. "Made sure no one saw," Roman said, taking the vines that wound up her spine. At the top of the vine, a small bud had grown and blossomed into a delicate black flower.

Nodin looked at the flower under her skin, missing the violent voice in her head. A small blue butterfly drifted in the window, sneaking through the slightly ajar window pane. "Is that one from the cave?" Roman asked, watching it flap wildly through the air towards them.

"No, its different. Look." Nodin pointed to the darker blue spots on its sharper-shaped wings. The butterfly landed on Nodin's outstretched hand, flapped its wings slowly several times, then exploded into a cascade of blue sparks.

Blooming from the sparks, a glowing mist hung in the air, an image scratched into it. The distinct details of the lake, their tree in the middle bloomed before them, the mist slowly drifting apart. "What was that?" Roman reached his hand out into the last remaining scraps of the mist as it floated to the floor. "We have to go." Nodin grabbed her coat from the pile of her clothes folded on the nightstand.

Nodin offered her hand to Roman, and gripping tightly she jumped them both to the lake. The moon sat high in the sky, a bright disk lighting the night. "Child," a quiet voice said from behind her, the wavering voice of an old man. Nodin turned to a tall gray-haired elf, his dark walnut skin showing his age. His long green robes did not shift in the wind whipping around them. "Hello," Nodin said nervously, her cadence coming out more like a question.

"You are lost, child." The elf's eyes rested on Roman who stood silently behind her. "I am building my own path." Nodin stepped in front of Roman, blocking him from the view of the elder elf. "You are going against your blood," the old elf snarled with an anger too harsh for his elderly body. "Which one?" Nodin challenged. "You see what they do," the elf waved his hand toward the land that the school stood upon. "Yes."

"How can you stand by?" The disgust etched into the elf's features so deep they appeared permanent. "The need to survive is strong," Nodin countered. While neither party was yelling there was no mistaking the battle that waged between them. "You insult your ancestors and what they fought for, what they sacrificed for." The elder elf stepped back, his robes barely shifting around him, turning away from her.

"Do not seek us when it gets dark, you are not of our world." He walked away from her, toward the lake. "You are right! I am not. I never was, not fully. I must balance my light and dark but you are no better for turning your back on me!" Nodin yelled at his retreating back. "You are not of my world," the elder elf repeated, pausing, "but you may be of the next world. You stand in neither world but maybe…" The elder elf stepped onto the surface of the lake, turning to her. The weave folded around the elf, before he disappeared his words echoed over the lake.

"A bridge."

Acknowledgments

To my Readers,

Thank you for joining me through this journey. As cliche as it sounds I could not have done this without you. Thank you for loving Nodin's rage just as much as me.

To my Beta Reader,

Maja you are so much more than just my beta reader. You are one of the first people I told about my book and understood the rage and got excited with me. Thank you for being a part of the team telling Nodin's story!

To my Husband.

Thank you for believing in me when I could not. I love you.

To EC Garrett

You have become a dear friend and colleague on this indie self-publishing journey and I thank you for being a light as we walk this path together.

To my Brother-in-law

For throwing a stink about not getting mentioned.

About the Author

Nesi is an indie author dreaming of bringing the worlds running rampant in her brain to life. When not writing Nesi spends her time reading and hoarding books like a dragon. Enjoying life with her husband, German Shepard mix and two spoiled cats.

Coming soon

Fractured
*A Split Between Magic
Novella*

1

Nodin's fingers hurt, the days old cuts had opened up again. She was done caring for this darn flesh-eating butyriboletus peckii. The raging mushroom had bitten her many times as she had tried to feed it the bloody strips of horse meat. Despite her elven lineage she was struggling with this plant. Two more weeks and she would be done with the thing. Third year was kicking her ass.

While she and her three roommates had fought their way through the school years, many had not made it. Nodin was sure at this point she knew everyone in her year by name.

Ascelin, Willow and Odette were not taking the advanced herbology class that Nodin had opted into this year. While technically it was a year four class, for the students who had chosen green for their aspect. Nodin had opted into the black aspect for her color. She had however challenged the course's entrance requirements, dancing her way through them. It had taken her until half way through her second year to full balance the use of her elven magic and keeping the school in the dark about her parentage.

Without Roman at the school any more she split her time between the lake and the hidden archive in the library. She visited Roman on the weekends. He had gone off to another school, the second level to the education needed to cast magic. While Briggems taught their students to cast in one aspect. Morrogets taught its students to cast in their second aspects and how to combine the two.

Only a small percent of graduating students pursued a second aspect, as an heir to was a requirement he did. He had chosen green for his second aspect. While it was a controversial choice when paired with his first aspect of black, Nodin thought it matched him well.

It was Thursday night and Nodin had been fighting with her fungus friend for over an hour to get it to eat. She was losing her mind, the blood that coated her hands long dried. "Nodin," Ascelin's angelic voice called from the main room of their dorm. She appeared in Nodin's doorway, while the girls did not know just how different Nodin was from them they took her in stride.

It had been a long time since they had questioned her mud stained feet, or plant covered room. After finding out about Nodin and Roman's romance that had started in her first year, they had stopped wondering where she kept disappearing to at odd hours.

The distance had put a strain on their relationship that had trampled through her second year till it had ended when Willow had yelled at the two of them when Roman had come to visit over Yule.

Which had led to a painful night of talking between the two of them. Which they had done in the cave at the bottom of the lake, it had helped them detach from the world around them and focus on their relationship. While they both still struggled with the distance from time to time, it was much better now. They had learned, and quite honestly they were both swamped with school that the time apart flew by.

"Joining us for dinner?" The girls still spent time with each other, while it was mostly quite studying in the living room they enjoyed each other's company. Nodin had discussed with Roman whether or not she should share her secret with them; she still had kept them in the dark. Waiting to see if their friendship lasted past their time together in school.

"Absolutely," Nodin wiped her hands on the towel, standing up. Ascelin wrinkled her nose at the singular fungi growing in the pot on Nodin's desk. The fungus stank of oxidized meat, which newly vegetarian Ascelin was struggling with the smell.

The group of women headed down to the dining hall. The grandeur of the gold wall, and tables of food had dulled in her years here. Nodin had found out earlier this year that all the uneaten food left over after the students had gone was packaged up and sent to local shelters and donation centers. It had eased her dislike of the abundance of food. Filling their plates up the women retreated to their favorite table.

Willow had a steaming bowl of peppery rabbit stew topped with cheese and sour cream, sourdough toast on the side. Odette had a plate of crying tiger beef, with a pickled cucumber salad. The variety of food still amazed Nodin to this day.

Ascelin had a cheese quesadilla, which she dipped into chili infused sour cream. Along with her quesadilla she had a large bowl of rice that she topped with butter. Nodin dug into her plate of roast yam spring rolls, and steamed onion scape boa buns.

Their table was alight with chatter as they watched this year's first year students gorge themselves on food. Nodin smiled at Ascelin as she came back to the table with lemon and coconut bars for the table. She had been in charge of picking the best dessert since their first year.

"You going to the library?" Willow asked as the women went their separate ways after dinner. "Yes," Nodin smiled at her friend. "May I join?" Willow followed her down the familiar hall.

Nodin watched herself in the mirrors, still looking for the void beast in the corners. It had been almost two years since the fight with Hester and the void beast had been absorbed into her. She missed the smoky voice in her head. Reminding her how sharp her teeth are.

Nodin hesitated, wanting to be alone. "Sure," Nodin smiled at her. "I need to research my butyriboletus peckii, it's not eating." School work it would be for the evening. She had hoped to spend the evening reading through the missing history of her people. "Perfect. Can I pick your brain about something?"

Willow prattled on about her struggles in her class. Nodin talked it through with her, helping Willow work through the issues she was having. Nodin was happy that she could help her friend.

~

Nodin rubbed her tired eyes, the text she was reading swimming off the page. It was a dull text on the use of black aspect magic. "What's your plan after school?" Willow was curled up in a chair, her book resting on her knees. Willow was beautiful in a southern Goddess way. She was tall and curvy, with a warm face she looked as though she was made by their Goddess in their own likeness. "What do you mean?" Nodin was confused where this question was coming from. "Are you gonna go back to school for your second aspect?" Willow worried her lip, a small pinch in her forehead as she reflected on the question she asked.

"I'm not sure yet," Nodin had not thought about it. Her plan had been to go to school to graduate then to slink back to her parents house in the woods. Past that she had no plan, and while the plan had not changed her life had. The plan may need to change. She had Roman now; and he had responsibilities as an heir. And one day he would take his seat and be running the political body.

How did she fit into that? "What about you?" Nodin distracted herself by asking Willow about her plans. "I'm not sure," Willow was lost in her own thoughts. "What about outside of school? What do you want to do with your life?" Willow needed the distraction herself. "Oh I have not thought about it. It's always been about surviving that I haven't planned any more," Nodin admitted. Willow knew about the loss of her parents, and attributed Nodin's struggle in life to that and not anything more. "What about you?"

"I am expected to go into my families business, but its not what I love," Willow sounded defeated. Willow's family made charms for sale. What Nodin knew about it, the family business was failing. "What do you want to do?" Nodin asked, watching her friend. Willow was a confident person, taking up all the space she needed in the world and not feeling bad about it. She was curled up in a ball looking unsure about herself. "I'd travel, and document all the creatures of the world," Willow smiled at the ceiling. "That sounds amazing," Nodin smiled at her friend.